IMPACT

Blue Blooded Brothers book 4

SOFIA AVES

First Edition

Cover Art by JS Designs Cover Art

Editing Services provided by A. Strom - Edits with a Coffee Addict

www.redpensandcoffeebeans.wordpress.com/

www.facebook.com/redpensandcoffeebeans/

Published by Little Quail Press

www.littlequailpress.com

ISBN 978-1-922448-19-4

CONTENTS

DEDICATION

Terry, Alyssa, Lila, Mandy, Lolo
and all my tribe
who constantly push the limits.
Never stop.

CHAPTER ONE

MICAH

Dirt spun past my ear as I pressed my foot down on the accelerator, releasing the brake with equal ease until the pedals sat evenly beneath my boot. The high-performance trucks ran rich in their track around the arena. Aggressively profiled tyres dug into the stadium's pack dirt, the lights hiding the crowd.

But they disappeared for me, as always.

Their roar had never affected me because I wasn't here for them. Two trucks passed me as I sat spitting dirt into the air behind my blue monster truck. Vibrations rumbled through me, despite the racing harness strapped across my chest. Sweat ran from beneath my helmet, my headset zinging static from the coordinators in the control room.

Benny wound a finger in the air above his head as he made room for my run.

"You're up, man. Don't overcook it," Benny's voice crackled over my radio.

I nodded into the gap, not taking my eyes off the dirt wall thirty feet in front of me. The brake slipped from beneath my foot, and I slammed the accelerator to the floor.

My monster revved like a newly released beast, the stadium dropping away entirely. Ben had made room behind me, but I didn't intend to backflip against the wall.

I wanted to balance two tyres right on top of it.

And that would take a lot of power and more than a touch of finesse.

The tyres powered at the base of the hard-packed mud wall. I knew every bump in it because I'd helped the track boys set it up two days before, adding my own custom designs and calculations.

We weren't racing for points; this was an exhibition ride for charity, with the singular goal to be as showy as possible. Still, a little technical work never hurt alongside it.

Benny would spot me from below and let me know if anything went awry. His judgement had always been sound, and I trusted his direction.

But the way I had planned my climb, I shouldn't need it.

The wheels articulated as my monster gripped the wall, climbing with each rev until the front wheels crested the top.

But I couldn't stop there.

I turned the truck, balancing the front end delicately while still powering the back wheels over the top until we sat diagonally on the top of the wall. Only the opposing front and back wheels touched the custom-made five-foot space at the top.

The roar of the stadium returned; fireworks Ty the Pyro — his title, not mine — had set up erupted on either side of the wall, showering my monster in sparks. At the height of their spray, I gunned the engine, and my monster leapt off the top of the wall.

My heart rate elevated as the long-overdue shot of additional adrenaline flooded my system, and for a long moment, I was aware of everything — the girls cheering behind the barrier set up to protect them, the crowd watching every moment with awe and glee. The stupidly bright lights heating the place to boiling point.

Jimmy, leaning well over the barrier, her mermaid-green hair swinging around her face as she watched me, attempting to avoid the other mechanics with little luck as they chattered at her from either side.

I blinked, leaving the adrenaline-fuelled moment I lived for, with a frown. Jimmy rarely came out of her section of the garage, though I knew she watched each lap like a hawk. She should; the only reason my blue monster ran so well, could only deal with what I put her through, was because of Jimmy's sharp eye and technical knowledge.

I was still watching her pale figure as she chatted away animatedly that the ground came up too fast. The front tyres contacted. I wasn't ready for it, my hands burning as the wheel skewed wildly in my grasp. I fought the steering as those same articulated wheels strained for purchase on the ground slewing beneath us. My neck jarred; I powered through the turn and put the truck into a controlled spin.

A yellow truck shot past me, and I knew I'd crossed tracks with someone else. Courtesy dictated each driver steer clear of another truck's trick, but I focussed on keeping my own truck intact. Apologies could come later.

Finally halting in the centre of a tornado of loose dirt, I smiled and waved at the crowd, irritated I'd lost my momentum, my concentration. Every time I got in the driver's seat, I chased that high for a few brief seconds, and now, it had evaded me.

Benny pulled up beside me in his own green monster truck, his hands spread wide.

"What the fuck, man? You nearly cleaned up Craig."

"I know," I said through gritted teeth, still smiling. "I'll do one more lap."

Benny frowned. "Take a break, man. Get Jimmy to check over your front end. You came down hard."

I knew that; my neck still ached from the pinch on contact with the ground. I just didn't need anyone else highlighting the fact I hadn't been in control for that moment. Adrenaline might be fun, but there was only one outcome I'd accept — the one I had aimed for, and I'd screwed that up.

Ignoring Benny, I picked up on the other trucks lapping the arena and chose a gap to slide between them, aiming for a long row of crushed cars. Dirt ramps bracketed the jump. It wasn't a hard one: the pitch had the potential for a high jump; always a guaranteed crowd-pleaser.

For the final time for the night, I gunned the engine, a whir that shouldn't have been there niggling at me from the front left side.

By the time my tyres hit the ramp, I knew I was good. Good speed, good line.

Then my tyres left the ground altogether, and I had another moment, staring out at the crowd.

People cheering, kids waving glow sticks. One girl flashed her boobs. I grinned; monster truck enthusiasts were a breed of their own.

My tribe.

The stadium and my warehouse were the two places my head completely cleared, where there was no judgement, and I didn't have to think about being *me*.

A man stood behind the woman who had covered her unleashed boobs, shifting into the light for a moment. My moment.

Pale, dead grey eyes stared at me, and my moment disappeared.

The distraction ate my seconds of flight as I stared, knowing who those eyes belonged to. Had last seen them in a bank rescuing a tiny girl from her madman father.

Joey was smaller, leaner than his brother, though both were supposed to be locked away, awaiting trial. How in the hell was he here tonight?

For the second time in one night, my tyres slid out from beneath me, my truck tumbling off the edge of the ramp at an angle it should never have landed at. Sand sprayed around me in a show of its own making while I shook my head, disgusted with myself. My truck slammed onto one side, skidding a distance until it stopped at the base of the wall I'd leapt off only moments ago.

I allowed irritation to overwhelm the growing unease in my gut, unwilling to face it just yet. Seeing the perpetrators who caused damage and spread fear was the reason I had become a cop in the first place. Especially when Cal had approached me when he formed the team heading the manhunt on Wayde Logan. If his brother was walking around the town, we had a whole lot of work to do — and questions to answer.

Grit speckled my vision as I hung from my safety harness and waited for someone to come and rescue me.

"The bearings are completely screwed, and you've wrecked the front end entirely. I hope you're up for a rebuild this weekend because you sure as hell can't expect me to fix that on my own. Not after I straightened the engine bay out the last time you rolled her. And did I mention ball bearings?" Jimmy planted her hands on her hips, her feet splayed, glaring at me.

I grinned; the girl hated working with bearings. She could fiddle with the finer points of a fuel management system all day. She would tinker with mechanical bits when she was bored, but those tiny ball bearings frustrated the shit out of her. It was like they had a personal vendetta against her.

"I wouldn't ever expect you to fix her on your own." I pressed my hand to the crumpled front zone, grateful Cal had signed off on the paperwork to help me get it road-registered. In doing so, I only needed to maintain one vehicle. "But I appreciate your help. Otherwise, I'd never sleep."

From the amount of damage I'd caused to my monster, it went without saying that no one would be sleeping for a long while. Her dented and cracked body filled my garage, obscuring half the sponsorship signs that decorated the walls and the desk Jimmy covered with new designs.

A collection of blankets huddled beneath the desk, ready for when she froze herself solid in winter. Jimmy insisted on working in icy conditions when the ideas in her head appeared faster than she could convey them to anyone else.

"Neither of us sleep." Jimmy rolled her eyes, green hair flying around her pale face. She gestured at my truck. "What– I can't begin to guess why — *how* — this happened. You're a better driver than this, Micah."

I opened my mouth to tell her I'd seen a man who shouldn't have been part of the general population, but her words struck home.

Neither of us got a lot of sleep; between her work at the track and on her own designs, Jimmy's insomnia came from somewhere deep within her, like she short-circuited when she slept. My mind wasn't as restless as hers; I just resented the time lost while inactive.

I held back a laugh; even I had to admit that was borderline the same thing. "You're right," I said, nodding.

Jimmy peered at me suspiciously, her hand sliding to her thin waist. "About what?"

"We both need rest. I'll get Craig to tow her home. I owe him after nearly running right over the top of him earlier. He likes money. It'll make him happy."

"That sounds too sensible for you. What's up?" Jimmy folded her arms, her red lips pursed.

I bit back the urge to tickle the shit out of her; she was so damn cute. "Nothing's up." The words came out sharper than I intended.

"You roll your truck, *again*. You screwed up a jump that I *know* you engineered to the finest degree and would never, ever fail to execute. You're lying to me. Where's my Micah?" Jimmy ticked off each sin as she listed them, glaring at me with hard eyes.

I swiped dirt from my face, sprinkling the cement floor liberally.

Jimmy huffed, her cheeks stained red. "I'll organise Craig *and* apologise to him for you. You. Stay. Here. And don't you dare move." She pointed at me.

"Sure, Tink." I slid my hands into my pockets and gave an easy shrug, ignoring the clenching in my gut at her words.

I'd rolled my monster months back, pushing too hard, and Jimmy had spent the week with me, fixing her. Danny pulled me up on it when he realised how little sleep she managed to survive on. It had sickened me that I hadn't realised what was right in front of me, especially since someone else had to point it out to me, and I refused to take advantage of her again.

Jimmy glared at me once more for using the fond term I'd always had for the tiny mechanic. She seemed to think she never fit in anywhere, though the garage may as well be her home — if she wasn't sleeping in my loft.

I waited for the usual argument that she didn't count as beautiful, like the fairy. Instead, she turned away, her hair swimming back, displaying the stain deepening on her cheeks.

Rocking back on my heels, I grinned as she left the garage in a huff, her usual habitat. Part of me wanted to catch her, to bring her back and finish the conversation properly — which may or may not involve kissing her — but I knew she wouldn't appreciate the contact.

The few times I'd brushed past her or had accidental skin-on-skin contact, Jimmy had leapt away. She didn't seem to have any personal aversion to me, though, as we'd been sharing a workspace for over two years. If she wanted to talk, I wouldn't push her until she was ready.

My smile slid from my face as I contemplated Joey. His appearance in the audience bothered me on too many levels, but the main one delved down into a degree of trust I never thought I'd question.

He hadn't escaped prison because every phone in the place would have lit up if either he or his psychotic brother were loose by their own design.

My boss, Cal, would never have the pulling power to release Wayde Logan's little brother. Nor would he ever let either of them roam free, given a choice, after the lives they had destroyed.

It wasn't his trust I questioned.

Joey's silent release would be a well-planned, perfectly executed event. Likely no one would be able to fathom the reasoning behind the ex-military man's actions.

I slid a hand over my truck, assessing the damage that the sight of the man had cost me. The pair of brothers had inflicted terror on nearly every team member who hunted them, extending well into their families.

Liam had better be sure about the path he had set us on.

CHAPTER TWO

JIMMY

I stalked out of the garage, leaving Micah smiling behind me. He seemed to think I missed his sense of humour, but the man didn't have a mean bone in his body. Paired with his faint smile and liquid brown eyes, I could rarely *get* mad with him, let alone stay that way for long.

I slowed my pace at the gated edge of the track. Benny and Craig dragged pieces of carnage from the arena. I recognised more than one piece that belonged to Micah's truck. A pang hit me; we had spent too many hours perfecting the custom-made truck for her parts to be scattered about the arena like junk.

Across from me, the cheer skanks hung out by the first garage — their usual hangout after events, before they inevitably picked a driver to go home with for the night.

After accidentally stumbling upon a head of blonde hair dropped to the crotch level of a local driver when I returned borrowed tech one night, I'd gladly opted — *pushed* — for the last garage when Micah picked me as his mechanic.

It isolated us from the rest of the mechanical teams, but even I still socialised with the boys on occasion.

The garage system was organised differently from any track I had worked at before. Each driver had his own permanent garage, providing their sponsorship or self-funded interest continued. That sponsorship also paid for a mechanic's services, or a team, if the driver required assistance to maintain his truck.

Other drivers, like Micah, were competent but liked someone to bounce ideas and theories with. He was my favourite type of driver to be paired with. The working relationship developed through our combined wins and fails.

"You've got a bit of work to do." Benny loped the last few steps across the arena, holding out a piece of body work.

I turned it around in my hands until the shape made sense to me.

"Yeah, I want that tape from the Control Tower later, so I can run over it all a few more times." I snorted, tucking the body work under my arm.

"Well, if you need help..." Benny offered with a grin, "Especially seeing as you do the lion's share in there."

"Are you kidding me?" my eyebrows hiked. "You know he doesn't sleep. The man never stops working, in one form or another," I grumbled.

"Sounds like someone else I know." Benny winked.

A blush ran up my cheeks; I hadn't realised anyone took that much notice of me. But it was a small community and a reasonably supportive one.

"I like getting my hands dirty," I raised my hands, showing him a single middle finger, the nail caked with grease and dirt.

"Watch out; your geek and tech will get muddled." Benny waved as he jogged back to help clean up the rest of the debris from the night's efforts.

One of the cheerleaders looked up as I pressed my hands to the railing, rising on the balls of my feet. Her gaze sharpened, shortening the distance, and I realised how I must look to her. Dressed in my usual black cargos and vintage Doc Marten boots adorned with hand-painted roses at the heel. My white tee was smudged with just enough grease that the L7 printed on the front was visible.

The cheerleader's gaze traced my five-and-a-half feet frame, and her knowing smirk gave me pause mid-jump.

Torn between wanting to help the boys and wanting to turn around and rant at Micah for wrecking his truck — and hide my pale backside in my garage — I hesitated a moment too long. Huge arms wrapped around me and lifted me off my feet.

I squawked, lashing out. My world blanked out, memory and my brain's protective measures screaming for safety I couldn't guarantee, especially after the total lack of physical contact for so long. Each hair on my arms raised, a prickling heat travelling up them as undiluted panic flooded my system.

The arms around me might be big, but they weren't big enough to be Micah. The man was a moving mountain, but he'd never picked me up before. My cheeks flushed at the thought amidst my panic that quickly bloomed into full-blown terror.

I'm safe. I'm safe. I'm safe—

I chanted the words in my head, a small gurgle forming in my throat. I clamped my lips shut, trying to push back the visceral reaction to human contact. Tears formed in the corners of my eyes.

Micah's soothing voice filled my head. I imagined his arms around me, and the panic eased, only to be replaced with a mocking voice, all too familiar in its measured insults. I shut it out, focussing on the image of Micah, his voice comforting as we worked side-by-side.

Not like that. Muscle bound behemoths oozing sexiness don't pick up pale, green-haired brainiacs like you.

Silver white hair flashed across my thin slice of vision as the arms whirled me in a circle, and I recognised my assailant. The clench in my chest eased, at least enough for me to swallow my scream.

"Danny. Put me–" my feet hit the ground, and I scowled up at Micah's best friend, who was almost as built as him but missed the bar by a lot on my Micah scale, "down."

"You are down, babe." He ruffled my hair, dropping a kiss to the top of my head. I rolled my eyes at Laura, who stood a few paces away.

"You need to stop manhandling her." She jabbed him in the ribs.

Danny doubled over, puffing. "Ow?"

"Ignore him," Laura advised, sliding an arm through mine. I jerked at the contact, my heart speeding up again, but Laura didn't seem to notice my reaction. Her gaze went over my head, into the arena as she towed me away from the fence. "He thinks because he's big, he doesn't need to abide by the rules of personal space. Like the rest of humanity does." She shook her head in disbelief.

"Hey!" Danny protested, jogging to catch up with Laura's speedy pace.

She reached his shoulder, and I reached hers — I got what she was doing, but next to the power couple they presented, I looked just as silly as I did if I stood beside Micah.

I resisted the urge to check over my shoulder to see if he had taken one of the cheer girls home.

Just.

"You don't have to pretend to be all friendly," I mumbled, studying the toes of my boots.

Laura halted, waving Danny off; he huffed at her and continued into the garage.

Micah emerged from the shadows, a filthy rag doing nothing to clean equally filthy hands. He had changed into his standard black tee, as custom made as his truck to fit his equally enormous body inside it. Dark hair draped in loose curls over his head, slicked back with a mixture of sweat and grease. A neat, short beard covered his chin. Even at this distance, he removed the rest of the world for me.

"I'm not doing anything for show, Jimmy," Laura said firmly, sliding her hand around mine.

I jolted a second time, my fingers flexing in an awkward motion.

"And I'm not a stray to protect." I couldn't take my eyes off Micah as he and Danny joked around, throwing air punches at each other.

"No. You're my friend."

"I am?" I responded by reflex, then closed my eyes. "Please strike that from the record. I'm gonna go hide in my work now." Could the ground open to swallow me in the presence of a tanned woman who was basically a mini goddess?

I might have been girl crushing on her, but there was no denying that Laura's toned legs and equally long, white-blonde hair far outclassed the cheer skanks. If they were put next to each other in a *who-wore-it-better* competition, Laura would win, hands down.

"Actually, we came to help you guys out. Danny's been...a bit antsy since Cal closed their investigation. Apparently, it's all done and dusted, and now they have nothing to do. Enforced holiday time does not sit well on a workaholic."

"I know what you mean." My eyes strayed back to Micah, who, oddly enough, stared back at us. I pasted a fake smile on my face, turning to Laura as though we were the besties she made us out to be. The weight of his gaze did strange things to my stomach. "Micah could use a little play time, too. And maybe a tow to get his truck back to his house."

Warehouse would be a better description for the enormous, empty industrial building Micah lived his spartan life in when he wasn't working or driving.

"He won't fix it here?" Laura frowned, craning around the boys.

Micah's blue monster sat forlornly in the centre of our garage, chunks of shredded fibreglass shell dangling from its mangled body.

I shrugged. "Maybe? Sometimes he leaves her here. Other times, he works on her all night, then goes to work while I keep going until she's good again."

Laura nodded as we reached the boys. Danny reached out instinctively to fold his hand around hers. Laura's body language softened at his touch, and I wondered if she knew she was doing it.

Probably. The woman reads other people as her day job.

It would be difficult to turn off, but then, both Micah and Danny did it as part of their job, too — Danny in his undercover stints and Micah as part of his team. I'd seen the way he interacted with the other members of his task force. Watched him gently push in a direction he wanted to influence the outcome of something with a glance or few quiet words.

"You done, bro?" Danny called.

Micah paused in his work, then placed his tools on the cement floor with a soft clang. I kept my head down for a minute, but I finally looked up at him after silence overfilled the workshop. He stared back, waiting as if Danny had spoken to me and not to him. My stomach flipped-flopped a little. I was used to our silent conversations, just not around anyone else. Micah's eyes were hooded, and it took him a moment to nod back to his friend.

"Yeah. Coming." He glanced at me again — not a sideways glance, but a full look they told me everything was *not* alright with him. "You want to come home and work on the monster with me?" he asked finally, a shadow grating beneath his usually deep voice.

"Nah, got shit to do here." I poked at my laptop, the screen lighting. I blinked, hoping I hadn't just given myself retina burn as Micah nodded and walked to his friends.

He looks like he needs the time alone.

I pushed the thought around in my head, mulling on it, but he had his friends and his monster. Those things alone kept him going. He didn't need me interfering with whatever he had planned.

I fiddled with my laptop, wondering why the boys weren't leaving, unwilling to roll out my things before they left for the night. The screen winked at me. I frowned, giving it the obligatory tap, and it came good.

"Do you need company?" a soft voice asked from behind me.

I started guiltily, swivelling to face Laura. "Oh, no. I work faster on my own, with no distractions." A wan smile made it halfway across my face before a yawn replaced it. I stifled it with a hand. "Sorry."

Exhaustion brewed by too many nights of deep-seated anxiety and memories that should have faded weighted me. Still, the moment I laid down, I knew my brain would be awash with new ideas. It was hard enough keeping track of the most recent ones.

Not sleeping until I had those cleared away might be the easiest path. Knowing Benny had noticed I barely slept was enough of a heads up to make me consider at least attempting to change my habits.

Micah never pushed the issue, one of the few like his, and I was grateful for it.

Laura waved my excuse away. "It's fine. You know we really are your friends, Jimmy. You don't have to pretend with us." She hugged me, drawing back to hold my gaze for what bordered on a too-long time.

I placed my feet in front of my pile of bags and gear, hoping she meant my across-the-arena run-in with the cheerleaders earlier.

Finally appearing to be happy with whatever she saw in my face, Laura hugged me one last time and trotted back to where Micah and Danny waited.

The three walked away from the garage, looking like a trio from some movie about friends or superheroes. One of the cheerleaders stepped out in front of Micah, her hands curling around his bicep as far as they went — which wasn't far —and chatting at hyper speed. Her hips swayed as she talked, and even I could see her movements were sinuous and sexy. My own limbs felt stumpy and awkward in comparison. I tucked them tightly to my sides.

Laura reached across Danny, touching Micah's other arm and together, they drew him away. The cheerleader folded her arms, sulking after them. Laura turned back to look over her shoulder at me with a quick smile. I waved, drawing the cheerleader's attention, who glared at me and stomped off in a huff.

I shook my head, pulling up schematics I had started a week earlier of an improvement on Micah's fuel distribution management system. Some tweaks could be made to improve power and efficiency. I ran each simulation, adjusting as I needed while the arena quietened around me. The last crew left the complex until the only light remaining came from my screen. Lines soon blurred before my eyes. I rubbed them and leaned back in my chair, stretching.

"Finished for the night?"

I opened my eyes, my second squark of the night echoing in the darkened space.

Joey grinned down at me, standing too close beside the gamer chair Micah had donated to me when he had realised how many hours I spent in it. A cheeky dimple I had a love/hate relationship with emphasised Joey's curled lips. I turned away from him and powered down my computer. Grey eyes lit up as I rose, his friendliness replaced with a hunger that brought too many emotions to the surface.

I shoved at his chest, the garage suddenly too small a space for two people, even ones as weedy as us.

Joey swayed backward but didn't move. He folded his arms over his chest, unmoved and still grinning.

"You need to take lessons in anti-stealth," I muttered as I zipped my laptop into its case and stowed it with the rest of my things. Joey followed my movements, but for once, I didn't offer any excuses.

Oddly enough, with him, as with Micah, I didn't feel the need to justify my existence. The comfort of a somewhat new but interesting friendship fell over me.

"Will never happen." He dangled keys from long fingers crusted with dirt. "Wanna go for a drive?"

CHAPTER THREE

MICAH

I walked through the quiet office space, working through how I would approach Liam. Waltzing into his office and demanding answers wouldn't achieve anything except a solid lack of communication in the coming months, and I couldn't afford that with Joey on the loose.

Getting Cal to speak on the team's behalf might be the better option. He had sent out a group message, requesting us off the short leave he'd provided; no other details. Which was typical of either of them, but he must have been taking notes from his mentor.

As a last-minute change to our enforced leave, it hadn't occurred to me that I might need rest to function fully today.

My night had been spent beneath my monster, trying to give her some affection while I went back over the night's drive in my mind. Jimmy usually sat through the replays with me, banging out ideas in the garage or at my loft. Picking out where I had stumbled, where I could improve, came naturally to her.

This time, I did it alone, inevitably returning to a familiar face in the crowd I had last seen through a spray of dirt — one who shouldn't have been there.

Several times during the quiet hours, I had called out to Jimmy, but the empty warehouse only echoed back at me. The girl worked at least as hard as me and rarely slept. Two insomniacs made for an interesting work marriage; we propped each other up when we crumbled and enabled our own bad habits through the small hours of the night.

But it was when I got most of my work done.

After Danny and Laura had dropped me off — Danny staying only long enough to help drag my truck to her home on the bottom floor of my warehouse — I worked on her until I had to wait for the fibreglass to cure. Still wide awake, I'd put my mind to work reviewing the ordnance for the task force.

I read through as many military and paramilitary newsletters as I could, looking for new tech to enhance our work. I shot off a quick email to Liam on a new laser-sighted scope, unsurprised when he replied minutes later, knowing he slept as little as the rest of us.

The few hours of rest I finally got were more than enough. I hit the gym on the bottom floor of our office building in Melbourne's CBD hours as the sun crested over the city, though Liam's car sat in its usual spot when I pulled in through the loading dock — the only entrance to the car park able to fit my now somewhat battered monster.

Weights had burned through my excess energy, leaving me with a clear head but the time I made it up to our glass bowl of an office. Before I had walked through the doorway, I already had an answer on how today might go.

Danny perched on the edge of my desk, a folder held loosely against his leg, Logan's photo paperclipped to the front. His shoulders were rolled back, relaxed, his man bun bigger than ever, I suspected, to further annoy Black. He raised an eyebrow in my direction, and a faint smile hid whatever churned about in a brain that worked faster than anyone's I'd ever seen.

Well, almost.

Which brought it all to the front.

"You know?" I asked, nodding to the file he dropped onto my desk. "Move your man cheek to your own desk, dude."

"Know what?" Danny obliged, sliding his ass off my desk. He twisted his wrist, so the file opened to Joey's photo and leaned back, giving me space.

I stared at Joey's fixed eyes, so like his brother's, and a measure of angst roiled in the depths of my gut.

Danny had been here, waiting for me with this file, the day after I'd seen the man. My mind began a rolling list of incidents, piecing them together to form a cloud of disquiet around me. Liam was conspicuous in his absence, considering he was the reason we were in the office during down time.

Cal had created issues with his ex-partner, Black, when he had sided with Liam over Ashley's temporary separation from her foster mother. I should have said something to Jimmy before I'd left the garage last night. Mistrust wrapped around me in an invisible cocoon. I rocked on my heels.

This style of mind-fuck was what made Wayde Logan so bloody infamous.

Liam had kept the task force together for more years than we should have been allowed. We had always put it down to his negotiating skills with the politicians upstairs. That and we had succeeded where so many prior units had failed. Though that was mostly because of Cal and Logan's mutual obsession with each other.

But that obsession had grown, overflowing into each of us, to some degree. Logan left no one untouched. I had thought I had escaped that notice, but now...?

Now, I already had doubts and could see the team crumbling around us. Not at the edges, but from within. A self-combusting mass dissolving from the inside instead of focussing on a common enemy we all knew too well.

And sometimes one we knew not at all.

I drew in a soft breath. "He's free."

"Who?" Danny's brow dipped, and his eyes slid to the photo he'd laid open, then back to me. He straightened from his slouch, his fingers nearly on the picture before he put it all together, swinging round to face me with bared teeth. "You've got to be shitting me."

"No one else would have the pull. I don't understand his direction." I mused as I ran every scenario through my mind to find Liam's motivation for releasing Wayde Logan's younger brother.

And for giving him the information that would put him squarely in my path.

Whatever endgame Liam had in mind could backfire on him in a spectacular fashion.

Danny eyed me, removing his hand from where it had drifted to the photograph on my desk. "Tell me."

My throat rasped slightly by the time I finished filling Danny in on the events of last night. I didn't offer any theories, as I had little information. Speculation only allowed for facts that filled the gaps in an incident, suiting them to a theory, rather than the other way around.

Danny tapped the file on his leg, a behaviour so reminiscent of Cal that I grinned.

He didn't.

"Why didn't you tell me last night?" he asked finally, his mouth pursed in a tight bow. I could almost see his mind churning over the information I had given him. Danny's brain worked faster than anyone's that I knew and that included Liam and Jimmy, though my mermaid mechanic came close to the geniuses I worked with. On the rare occasion she let her facade slip, I wondered if she might be concealing her full potential.

I shifted slightly, walking around my desk to turn on my terminal.

"Dude..." Danny's impatience bit through his words.

"Because I wasn't sure how to present the...encounter."

Because I wasn't sure what I thought I saw.

And that was a dangerous point.

"We could have had a look around together before they cleaned the arena. He might still have been there." Stress replaced the impatience in my best friend's voice.

"He wouldn't have stayed," I said the words softly, firmly, but my stomach clenched all the same. "Liam called us together. We wait."

Should we have stayed? Had I left Jimmy working on her simulations with the brother of a psycho wandering around her workplace? I shook my head to clear it, but the need to know she was safe speared through my thoughts.

A tang of metal coated my tongue as I fumbled for my phone and sent off a message to her. Jimmy didn't have a phone, but she usually hooked into the track's internet, courtesy of Benny and the Control Tower. The boy knew everything that went on at the track, practically lived there.

Jimmy still hadn't responded. I placed the phone on my desk and stared at it.

"She'll be fine." Danny's hand on my shoulder brought little comfort. I nodded and pretended that it did, though I knew he would see through it. "You're almost as fast as Liam."

That got a laugh, but not from me.

"No one is as fast as Liam. In most things," Cal grumbled as he slung his gear onto his chair with a nod in our direction. He sorted through a well-worn leather satchel and extracted a sheaf of files. "We're reorganising. For now," he raised his voice to cover Danny's instant protest. "Weapons Trace task force. I thought you," he waved a manilla folder my way, "and Ally might lead on this one. It's right up your alley and hers. Dirty cops."

"We're not Internal Affairs," Danny protested as he slipped a file from Cal's hand, "this isn't what we do."

Cal closed his hand on empty air and looked down. "Damn, Danny. Too fast, man." His compliment was rewarded with a quick grin from the young cop. "But taking on a new case prevents us from being disbanded now Logan's away."

Danny shot me a quick glance. "Is this why Liam called us in?"

"No." Cal grimaced. "I'm not sure what else he needs. He's been...evasive."

"When is he not?" My snort transformed into a fake cough. "So– leading?"

"It will suit Ally, and she'll need your technical knowledge. Both of you." Cal held my gaze steadily. "Danny, you and Brett will mentor them both on undercover work and setting up an investigation."

Danny nodded curtly; his attention already invested in the information before him.

"Thanks," I answered for both of us. I stepped back to give Danny the room he would need to work through how he wanted to play the information. It might have been my lead, but going in without the best strategy around me would be a dumbass decision — and an egotistical one.

The sort of decision that always cost the team in one form or another.

The office settled as each of us focussed on our own headspace. The file wasn't a thick one; there was only enough information to be pertinent. One Captain Travis Nelson had been flagged after a cache of missing weapons had turned up on the local black market. And on more than one occasion, that funded potential crime rackets and armed drug dealers.

There were some gang issues, but they weren't the focus of the case. Nelson also had a lot of his cops logging big hours but had little to show for it. I half snorted at the page; we had hunted Wayde Logan for almost five years without much to show on a daily basis. The manhunt had logged a shit ton of hours, but we'd made the difference up at the tail end of the investigation.

My thoughts floated back to Joey as I flicked through profiles on the cops. Each one was dirtier than the prior, with small warnings Nelson had shunted to the proverbial bottom of the pile to disappear off the record. Some of the notes told me Ally had already done a little digging.

Time theft was a costly issue in government departments — hours logged but never worked. Nelson's precinct had logged enough to cover his own wage more than nine times over in the space of a year. There was an incident involving false evidence being planted and a list of anonymous call outs for gun seizure raids that had turned up very little.

"You two start the investigation on your high horses. Make them hate her. You get friendly with at least one of them on the geek side of it. You're a weapons specialist. Make that an appreciative and valuable commodity. That way, when you eventually accept the offer of acquiring something nasty, they'll trust you and have a laugh at turning someone straight like Ally crooked." Danny thumbed through my file and slid a photo from the back.

"Ugly bastard." I studied the man whose face looked like it had been squashed against a door too many times. His grimace at the camera made me think he might have been.

"Just a bit. Greg Pearson. Looks like your sort of man — local shooting club championship. Got into a bit of trouble a few years back for working on demolitions he shouldn't have. Brought a building down under observation but used excessive force. Cleaned up the side of a takeaway shop across the street that had been evacuated, thank God."

He flicked another photo out, making a fan of the people he had identified.

"Yeah, I can see how that could work. I'll need tutoring. My poker face is pathetic."

"I know. We got you, boo."

"Thanks." My phone buzzed across the desk. I returned my attention to it, but it was just an email from Benny on the next meet.

C'mon, Jimmy.

The girl was likely asleep. I hoped she hadn't passed out over her work in the garage. I'd found her that way once, her green hair falling between the gaps of her keyboard. The place had hit below freezing overnight. I had covered her with my jacket and added my shirt when she started to shiver.

Her lightweight form lacked physical muscle tone that she made up with her thought process and determination to see a project to completion. A two-seater sofa had arrived the next day, along with a bundle of blankets she had taken ownership of, almost immediately.

Danny nudged my phone. "You wanna go check on her?"

"Nah, I'm good. She'll be fine." But I checked my phone again, anyway.

Danny snorted, muttering something about mother hens. He slipped back to his desk, typing as fast, though he was unlikely to keep up with his brain.

Cal filled the room with the scent of burnt coffee that neither Danny nor I drank since it screwed with our workouts. And his sleep pattern.

It was hard to screw with something you didn't have.

Despite my efforts to hone my body and mind, the practice of relaxing enough for sleep to come naturally instead of through a joint combination of physical and mental exhaustion eluded me.

As it did for Cal.

When I'd worked out my boss' nightly habit of staying awake to search for Logan, I organised enough tech for him to work from home rather than skulk around the office at all hours of the night.

I figured that if Cal worked from home, he might get some sleep instead of trying to drive himself home under crippling emotional stress. We all had our obsessions, but Cal's drove him to the edge. It was only after we had caught Logan that Cal realised we all knew of his.

The extra surprise for him had been that we were okay with it.

Cal sighed, draining his mug. I caught the ceramic before it slid off his desk.

"I'll make you another," I offered.

Cal nodded; his bloodshot eyes told me he wouldn't argue, though a new obsession drove him now. With his focus shifting to Mila and their pregnancy, frantic energy swarmed about him, and I could only imagine what he must be like at home. I had stepped in early on in his obsession with Logan to help, but this was entirely a different matter.

Cal's love for her and the baby drove him, and the best we could do was support the shell of the man who came in every day, even when he didn't need to.

I refilled his cup and went back to work.

"You going for *employee of the week*?" Theodore Black glared at me as I walked into our small kitchen with Cal's mug for the third time.

"Would you like one?" I offered with a grin.

Black stared at me with hard eyes, then shook his head. "Fuck me."

"Nah, I have other prospects."

Black snorted, akin to a laugh for him. I grinned while I searched in the fridge for the leftovers of my mother's most recent feast.

She always made enough for an army — so when I collected food from her, she made five times as much, convinced we couldn't look after ourselves and were starving.

Seeing as she was the best cook any of us had ever met, no one argued, and the excess food disappeared in a hurry.

I pulled out a tray of handmade gnocchi, spooning it into portions that would fit into the microwave.

"You're not our caterer. Or our coffee boy. You know that, right?" Black asked from behind me.

"You're not going all fatherly on me, or are you seducing me with those words?" I asked, concentrating on not making a mess.

Black snorted. "Between you and man bun-boy over there," he gestured out of the kitchen in Danny's direction, "we have enough testosterone to fill a city building."

"Nah, you've got that covered all on your own. Here." I passed him a bowl and a fork.

"Thanks." Black hoed into his food. "Make sure you feed him extra. He's still not sleeping. Neither is Mila, but that happens. He's just got to accept he can't fix it for her and just needs to be there. And he refuses to marry her yet, which means I'll have to step in soon." He shook his head, filling his mouth with more food than should have reasonably been able to fit inside it.

I took Cal's bowl to his desk. Snores emanated from a jacket covered bundle in his chair.

"Don't wake him," Danny hissed.

"Wish I could have a day nap." I backed away, grumbling playfully.

Black placed bowls on both our desks.

"Thanks, Dad," we chorused. Danny reached back for a knuckle bump; I obliged.

"Like fuckin' Maverick and Goose," Black groaned, sinking into his chair.

"He's Goose." Danny and I pointed at each other, laughing.

Black shook his head, leaning back.

Cal woke long after we finished eating, accepting the cold bowl of food, and ate silently. Ally joined us; her usually perfectly-pressed white suit slightly crumpled. For once, her hair perched on top of her head in a tight knot. Pages turned behind me in the same pattern as I had done hours beforehand.

Though she had been with us for nearly six months, she was still the team's newbie despite her success with a test case Danny had set her up with after her somewhat magnificent failure in Internal Affairs.

She sat silently at her desk, clicking away mechanically with the rest of us, who had nothing real to do but wait for Liam's summons.

I focussed on researching an automated grenade launcher hosted by a drone the US Marines were looking at adding to their units. It would be a great incentive in getting Nelson's demolitions enthusiast to trust me. I pulled up as much information as I could on the man. Greg Pearson might be ugly as hell, but he had links in a few of the same organisations as I did. That could help generate his trust.

The more I studied his profile, the more I thought the grenade launcher would be perfect. Maybe I could convince Liam to spring for one. I also wanted to look at incorporating a canine unit into our raids. But my gaze kept creeping back to the folder with Joey's picture where it had migrated to at the bottom of Danny's inbox.

The elevator doors pinged open, and Liam strode through as though he had been walking the entire time. His momentum failed to hide the extra body exiting the lift, and the knot of disquiet in my gut tightened.

Two pairs of grey eyes varying in intensity stared at us through the glass walls. One, familiar — that I saw every day — had trusted my life and career with countless times. The other, I knew only from the bank, when I'd taken Ashley back from his madman brother.

And from last night.

Cal half rose, his mouth open to rip Liam a new one while his hand hovered over an empty holster.

"This'll be interesting." Danny leaned back beside me, his arms folded.

I nodded my agreement, dividing my attention between the insurgents and the incident room.

Black looked at Cal, not even watching the potential shit-show walking in the door, his attention fixed on his ex-partner. His hands hung open and loose at his sides.

Ally's eyes narrowed. She lifted her giant pink travel mug, which effectively hid whatever expression she failed to repress. It was a good fall back while the girl trained, but she'd need to manage to hide her opinions in a better way. Danny would teach her if the team held together long enough to allow it.

Liam stopped in the doorway, his back to Joey, making eye contact with every member of the team. The thinner man lurked behind him. When Liam's gaze found mine, he held it for a long, silent moment before moving on. A shiver I didn't bother to conceal raised the hairs on my arms.

"I'd like to introduce you to the newest member of the team."

I waited to hear jaws hit the floor, but the only sound was Cal's teeth clicking sharply together.

34

CHAPTER FOUR

JIMMY

The ground rushed up at me; vibrations ripped through the body of the well-loved WRX Impreza, transferring to my bones. Dirt burst over the bonnet, hailing the windshield in pebble-studded clods that bounced off the sides as Joey swerved around a boulder. He wrenched up the handbrake, the car skidding and slithering to a stop in a shower of dead leaves and looked across at me, his eyes sparkling.

Unkempt, dirty blonde hair stuck out at different angles, hiding the sharp lines of his face. He had a watchful quality about him, but when Joey smiled, his whole face lit up, energised.

"You're supposed to stay on the road, you know." I pointed at a dusty trail that disappeared between the gum trees ahead.

"It's more of a track." Joey grinned, putting the car into gear. "You wanna go again?"

I looked out the window at the failing light with a sigh. "I have to get back. Micah's driving tonight. He might need me."

Light fingers brushed the back of my hand where I had half-tucked it beneath my knee. I flinched, unable to prevent the cold sweat that beaded my skin instantly, twisting back to Joey. He hadn't moved, but the air evacuated from between us.

"Emphasis on *might*," Joey said in a quiet voice. "Come back and shower at mine. It's cleaner than the bathroom at the track."

"Anything would be cleaner than that," I agreed wryly, rubbing my hand over the patch of skin that prickled from his touch.

But anything is better than nothing.

If I kept distracting myself, maybe one day I would behave like a regular person and have a real life with a home. To be able to function when another human touched me without freaking out.

He traced over me with his eyes, which felt more like a caress. Trying to sit still under his intense gaze, I studied every part of his face, but the distraction didn't work; something kept drawing me back to those eyes.

I need to be normal.

It's normal to be in a car with a friend. It's normal to have contact with other people.

My mantra never worked, but habit turned it into a prayer sent to a deity I didn't have faith in. But though jerky, neither Danny nor Laura's contact had felt quite like his. My mind drifted to Micah, but I yanked my thoughts firmly back to the present. He was a friend, a good friend, but one I kept secrets from.

And that had to be how it stayed.

Joey leaned back a little, giving me as much space as he could.

Offering a wan smile, I shivered, then realised he was touching my hand again, the barest contact.

"Okay. Yes. Let's do it." Do what? What had I agreed to? Ah, the offer of hot water and a sanitary place to wash. Yes. I was all up for that.

I blinked, pulling myself back from my meandering, distracted thoughts a second time.

"Good." Joey removed his hand from my frozen one, revving the battered rally car.

Dust and leaves scattered the trail in our wake.

Hot water streamed down my back. I washed my hair with the shampoo and conditioner Joey had provided, locking the door. It hadn't seemed enough, but I couldn't find anything else to barricade the door. I kept an eye on it, instead, as steam curled around me, a welcome neighbour as my head cleared, the heat draining tension from my back.

Joey had instinctively given me space, seeming to know my story without me speaking the words. I was grateful, never being one to share much about my life before yesterday, *any* yesterday, and the illusion of temporary safety crept over me.

I stepped out, enjoying the luxury of a fresh, clean towel, and found a folded set of clothes that weren't mine, though they did have my name on them.

Well, pinned to them. I read the note over three times, stifling laughter.

Take the clothes, Mech-girl. And leave your old ones to wash. I'll trade them back later.

I grinned. Joey knew I would never take charity, but by offering to wash and trade them, it felt like I would be giving them back at a later stage, though I knew he would refuse them.

The back of the note felt rough. I turned it over, laughing outright this time.

Seriously, Mech. Take the clothes.

I put the note down, turning away from the mirror, though I knew it would only reflect clear, pale skin.

A little *too* pale because I spent too little time in the sunlight. Getting outside with Joey blinded me for the first few minutes. But the afternoon sun warmed me, a reminder that being whole again might just be possible.

I grabbed the new clothes, slipping the Black Sabbath tee over my head. It fit a little too well, but who was I to argue with a vintage tee? Suppressing a grin, I bundled my well-worn clothes in my arms and unlocked the bathroom door.

"We should invite some of the other drivers out next time. See if we can get a little competition going." Joey pulled a jacket over his grey shirt when I walked into his living space. He pointed at a folding door. "Laundry tub's over there."

"Thanks." I nodded, but he waved the gesture away as though it were nothing.

Maybe to him, but it was a big step for me. Accepting *anything* was a big step for me, though something told me he wouldn't expect anything in return.

Air whooshed from my chest. The last time I had trusted someone like that, it had cost me more than a simple exchange.

"Don't stress it, Mech-girl. Someone's gotta look out for you."

"I prefer to fly under the radar." I said, then closed my eyes. "Sorry, I-"

Joey waved my comment away a second time. "All good, babe. So, what do you think about some company on our drive?"

"Maybe." I frowned.

Trusting Joey came on in a bit of a rush when he had appeared at the garages a week ago. It had been so long since I trusted anyone that I refused to share that step towards intimacy with other people yet.

"Benny? He's good value. Craig's always up for a laugh," Joey continued, ruffling his hands through his hair, so it stuck up at crazy angles. He grinned, and the dimple returned. "Micah?"

"Not Micah," I answered automatically. Too fast. I cringed, backing away with my hands raised. "Sorry. That came out wrong. He's my friend, but-" My mouth dried. Trying to explain my reasoning brought on more panic.

"It's fine." Joey didn't move, didn't encroach on the space I put between us, his voice light. "Not a social girl, huh?"

Not social, not a girl, just a shell of a person who used to live in my skin.

"Invite whoever. I'll fix whatever they break." I grinned, my smile strained at the corners, pushing my qualms aside.

At some point, I had to live again. Why not start now?

Joey nodded slowly, sliding his hands into his pockets. "You know you don't have to serve everyone, Jim. Let them fix their own shit for a while."

"That's a novel concept." I snorted.

"Let them," Joey coaxed. "Laugh with the rest of us over the little things. I bet-" he flicked off the lights of his small apartment, "that you can beat my time on a lap."

The track we had attacked were fire trails in a national park outside the city. We weren't technically supposed to be on them, but the afternoon had been relaxing.

"Alright," I agreed, combing through my hair with my fingers. "I'll give it a shot."

"You'll be great, babe." Joey grinned, then looked away, extending his hand, his palm facing up. A fine-toothed comb sat in it.

I stared at it for a second, then quickly combed my hair, removed the few sea-green strands, and put it back in his hand.

Joey nodded, pulling the door open without a word.

Crowds packed the arena when we pulled up at the back. Joey gave me a quick grin and wandered off to a group of men hanging out into the car park. I slunk into the back of the garage complex, letting myself in with a combination code.

Micah's legs stuck out from beneath his monster, which listed slightly to one side.

"What happened to...did you have to *tow* her back here?" I asked, incredulous. Scratches not from the previous night decorated one side from top to tail. "Seriously, what the hell did you do to her, run her down a hill on her side?"

Micah had covered them with corporate logos, some older ones from companies who no longer sponsored him. I kicked at his feet when he didn't answer me, huffing.

"She's fine." Micah wheeled his way out from underneath his truck, a small smile on his face. "A little battered, maybe. Took her for a drive after. Danny helped me put her back together. I used your email for a work thing."

"That's fine," I answered, then rethought my words. "What's *not* fine is that you think it's okay to keep trashing her, night after night. One day, she won't work when you need her." It came out a hell of a lot snarkier than I meant it to, but as my eyes tracked over the listing vehicle, I realised there was a whole lot more damage than I had initially thought.

I opened my mouth to argue, but Micah beat me to it.

"Took her out for some fun on the beach. Did a hill climb, but we didn't quite crest the top the way I had expected."

I stared, my mouth hanging open. "'*I didn't*' isn't in your vocabulary, Micah."

Right alongside "I can't", "I won't", and "it's impossible".

"Sometimes we make mistakes." He slid the board out from beneath him, pulling his knees up to lean over them. "I'm still learning."

"Bullshit." I snorted. "You're one of the best drivers I've ever met. Precision and efficiency fuels you, I swear. You're a crappy liar, even if it's just to yourself. But she's not drivable, Micah. Not tonight."

You'll get hurt, and I'll have to watch.

I could help him repair his truck, but I couldn't help him repair his body.

"She'll be fine." A mulish look drew lines on his face I had never seen before.

"Keep saying that, and maybe it will come true." I pressed my lips together.

Micah didn't move, but something in his positioning changed.

I leaned forward, pressing my elbows to my knees, returning his study. The mulish lines settled back into smooth planes. High cheekbones any woman would love to have, drew attention to dark, liquid eyes that stared right through me. It had taken a little to get used to, but Micah observed, took in the world and the people around him.

If they disagreed with him or did something he didn't like, he never said anything, content to be a lone satellite that did his own thing.

Usually.

He broke our impasse first.

"You're wearing something different." He nodded to my clothing.

A small laugh escaped my lips before I could clamp them shut again. "That's what you're leading with? My clothes?"

Silence met my comments.

I sighed, hanging my head between my knees. Bare, utilitarian concrete stared back. The hard surface indented the muscles of my back, just as the innards of Micah's monster became a map in my mind, I'd spent so many hours staring up at it.

"Lemme have a look at her; I'll see what I can fix." I pushed the emotional stuff aside. It had no place in a room made for analytics and improvement.

"We don't fight. Why are we fighting when you have new clothes?" Micah asked softly, his voice near my ear.

I raised my head and realised he had scooted closer while I indulged in self-pity mode. A shiver ran over me at his nearness, and for the first time, his closeness was welcome.

"No, we don't fight." I agreed. "We work."

A small smile tugged at the corners of his lips, his eyes lighting up in a language we both understood.

"Then let's work."

CHAPTER FIVE

MICAH

Joey's appearance on the team threw us all into a head spin. Liam could have scalped Cal on the spot, and the tall man wouldn't have stopped his headlong charge across the room. One word from Black, however, had.

"Mila," Black squeezed Cal's shoulder hard enough to strain his shirt across his chest. "Trust he knows what he's doing." He aimed the words at his ex-partner, who nodded, some of the frantic energy sinking away from Cal's frame. The look Black shot to Liam, however, was nothing short of violent.

"Trust is a good term," Liam mused, sliding his phone out of his pocket, "I believe that's what teams are built on."

The moment he had stopped speaking, his attention was already on the tiny screen. Liam strode out of the office, leaving us with the man who had dropped Danny and kidnapped Mila the last time any of us had seen him.

He offered a pasty, weak smile. I was surprised he didn't wave.

Trust came at a price; one I doubted Liam had anticipated. As we grudgingly gave a measure of it to Joey, to follow instructions, albeit poorly, it eroded from our combined faith in Liam.

Not to mention the scatty impact it had on the rest of our duties. Putting together a half-assed investigation was likely to get Ally and me halfway to killed. Especially with the targets we had painted on our back going undercover together — even if it was as ourselves.

"You want what information?" Captain Travis Nelson stared insolently at Ally, a smirk I wanted to swipe from his face tainting the corner of his too-thin lips.

Straight shouldered, Ally swished her curtain of white-blonde hair behind her. "I need your records on these case files and any...remaining details on evidence submitted here." She held out a sheaf of papers. Nelson's red-rimmed eyes flicked to me and back.

We had decided to go with Danny's plan. Ally would lead, as too many people knew she had worked Internal Affairs for that to change. I'd appear as her muscle-back up, the dumb grunt with the pretty partner.

She had made me promise to check out her profile obviously and to take a back seat. It gave me the perfect opportunity to work on softening up Nelson's men, and I'd found that people talk far too much when you made an effort to listen to them.

"Yeah, love. Sure. I'll get them to you. Next week, maybe." Nelson passed the papers off to a uniform without looking at him, and there was a distinct thump as the fake request forms hit the bin. "Anything else?"

"Oh, I would hate to have to hand something else to you, Travis." Ally sidled up to him, stepping into his space.

Nelson straightened, one foot scraping back an inch. Ally's voice was sugar-sweet. "Like a subpoena."

Nelson's already sour face tightened.

I bit back a laugh. Ally's months of talking shit in our office were already paying off. The girl had a hell of a backbone; appeared to thrive on the buzz she got from the conflict.

"Fuck me," a sweaty body thumped against the desk I leaned back on, "would you look at that."

I didn't need to look at the uniform. "Yeah, she's a pretty one." I nodded noncommittally. Greg Pearson had only just gotten on my radar, and I already detested him.

My mark let out the loud laugh I had wanted to only a moment before, but for a vastly different reason. "Yeah, you with her *with* her?" He faced me, wiggling his eyebrows in my peripheral vision.

I didn't look at him in case I punched him.

Time to play the part.

"Nah. I'm an ass man. This view works just as well." The words stung my tongue with a bitter flavour I doubted would wash off easily.

Danny had warned me that with each undercover role he played, he lost a little part of himself. I knew he was glad to be driving a desk now since he had Laura, but I also knew he was in his element doing this sort of work.

It wasn't mine.

"Bit of a hoity-toity bitch, huh?" Greg didn't bother to lower his voice, his stale body odour wafting over me.

I gritted my teeth. "Yeah, I'd love to shoot her with one of those new grenade launchers. The Mark 19 USMC are using. You seen that?"

"Hell, man. I've shot one. You wanna have a play?" Pearson's expression shifted, and we were off.

I washed my hands clean of grease — both the metaphorical sort and the physical goo — only minutes before Craig arrived in the garage.

"You're up, man." He wheezed breathlessly, staring at the bits and pieces of my monster dismembered on the floor. "I tried the radio, but no one picked up. Ahh– that is, if she's going?"

"She's fine." I quelled laughter at the look Jimmy shot me from beneath her lashes.

Damn, but he was cute when she was angry. But not half as cute as when she discussed a new theory or explaining schematics she'd dumped directly from her brain onto her screen. Or any scrap of paper floating about our garage. Occasionally, the walls.

"She's light. Don't do anything that requires balance. We haven't tested anything." Jimmy swiped a filthy hand across her brow that left a dark stain on her pale skin. She threw a rag down with the rest of the garbage and stalked out.

I frowned over Craig's shoulder as she stomped away. We hadn't talked after she had — rightfully — ranted at me. The last woman who had given me a piece of her mind was Gina. And I didn't want to ever relive that break up. She had hated the hours I spent at the track, hated the hours I spent at work. She hated pretty much everything about my life but the sex.

"You're up," Craig reminded me.

I nodded without looking at him, hearing the urgency in his voice, but my feet didn't seem any more inclined to move than the rest of me.

Green flashed amongst mechanics and crews she didn't often socialise with, and a familiar shape blocked my view of her. My teeth ground together as I watched his shaggy head dip, his hand on the small of her back.

Doesn't he know she hates other people touching her?

Jimmy moved, and I half expected her to punch him; I *definitely* expected her to shy away from the contact. The girl hated crowds; for all the hours I had spent with her, I had barely touched her. Something about her just gave off that vibe that said she didn't want anyone in her space.

Jimmy looked up at Joey, her head tilted back as she laughed, a smile spreading across the portion of rounded cheeks I could see.

What the actual fu–

I spun on my heel, nodding to Craig, who backed away. Benny looked up from his own work, his brow creasing a little. He raised an eyebrow, but I waved him away. I didn't need a mirror to tell me what my face looked like; his retreat said everything.

I couldn't work out why Jimmy apparently felt so much safer with a man who had attacked so many, who she had only just met.

And not me.

My drive passed in a blur. I'd watch the recording later, pick out the flaws, what could be improved. All I wanted was to get back to the garage and talk to Jimmy.

I trundled my monster at a snail's pace along what passed for our pit lane, holding my hand out the window to high five anyone hanging out along the fence line and whoever could reach.

Normally, I interacted with the crowd, especially on charity nights. This time around, I ran on automatic, with two thoughts running through my head.

What hellish game is Liam playing putting this tool in my space?

Why doesn't she trust me?

I couldn't fight with whatever Liam had set up, at least, not yet.

But I *could* work out what was going on with Jimmy.

I had worked with the girl for nearly three years, living in each other's back pockets. She slept at my house often enough to be a best friend or even a girlfriend, but the more I thought it through, the more I realised I had no concept of where our relationship stood.

Part of me wanted to call Laura. Her coaching style appeared to have helped Danny focus on life rather than skittering at its edges, but I knew that would be the coward's way out.

I generally stayed out of other people's shit, preferring to let them handle it. If they wanted comfort or help, most people I considered friends — the men I worked with and one mermaid girl, plus a plethora of family — usually asked for help. Or just started talking.

I sighed, running a hand through my hair. Sweat and dirt crusted it. I shook my fingers through it but only succeeded in adding smears of mud to already greasy fingers. A shower could wait until I spoke to Jimmy first.

Which would be hard to do.

When I pulled into my garage, it only held one body. One far too tall, and it didn't have green hair.

"Where is she?" I didn't bother to soften my tone as I swung down from the cab of my truck.

"Off. Having fun." Joey smiled, but it didn't reach his eyes.

Creepy fuck.

"So, she's working, then." I turned my back on him.

Not the smartest thing to do, but Liam had pushed him in my direction, and I needed to trust the man who had headed up the hunt for Joey's brother.

But now that hunt had ended, with Logan awaiting trial, and our job stopped there. Why Joey had been sent to me was a mystery. One I needed to solve, and soon.

"The girl knows how to have fun without slaving away for you." Joey's voice was laced with derision.

I blinked. "What do you know about my mechanic?"

"Is that all she is to you? No wonder she needed to get out and relax."

"She does relax. When she's working and designing. It's what she loves." My jaw ached. I pried my teeth apart and swung back around. "Seeing as you've just arrived, you wouldn't know that about her."

You know nothing about her.

Reigning back my urge to find a rocket launcher and send the douche into orbit, I smiled, channelling my inner

Danny. Still, I had no idea how he fell into the roles he played so naturally. I needed coaching. Maybe I should take lessons from him with Ally. My own anger bubbled beneath the surface, where it usually stayed, but for now, it was no longer dormant.

"Have I just arrived, though?" A light glimmering behind his eyes, Joey wandered over to Jimmy's desk and fidgeted with her things.

I pressed my fists to my back, forcing the facade over my features.

Stay out of everyone's life.

But this time, I couldn't.

"Take your bullshit out of here. Jimmy's probably at home, sleeping off a week of charity exhibitions. Unlike you, she works her ass off."

"Because she needs it." Joey assessed me, his eyes tracking over my frame. The smallest hint of a smile curled the corner of his lips. "You don't know, do you?"

"Know what?" I frowned; the words slipped out by reflex. I cursed myself for giving away any point of weakness.

Joey just smiled.

I gritted my teeth; if he didn't want to spit out whatever rubbish he had in mind to say next, I couldn't force him, though the idea had merit. I brushed my fingers over the shape of my phone in my pocket but seeing as Liam had given me the look when he introduced Joey to the team, I figured I should be working on this one alone.

"Are you going to make yourself useful?" I asked, trying to keep my tone light.

Joey's grin widened.

Fail.

"J! Did you want to–" Jimmy flounced into the workshop, her green hair flying around her face. She stopped when she saw me, slowing to stand next to Joey. "Hi."

Awkward.

I nodded. "Just cleaning up. Thought I might tinker for a few hours. Next show isn't for another week."

I left it an open invitation, as I always did with her. And she always accepted the offer without saying anything. Instead, she talked to me about some new concept that had filled her amazing brain in the hour since I last spoke to her.

"Oh, we– I, um." She looked hesitantly up at Joey.

He stared back at her, his face softening as he muttered something I couldn't hear.

I grabbed my tool bag from under the bench where I had stowed it next to Jimmy's laptop bag and her pile of blankets. An ever-growing collection of schematics were slotted between them.

The bag was heavy enough that I could drag the waxed canvas across the floor. The metal inside scraped and clanged on its short journey. I planted myself at my truck and tried to ignore the fact I'd just had a temper tantrum in my garage — albeit a mostly silent one — and began to fiddle. I immersed my head in a very blurry picture of the night's drive.

I'd have to look up the recording the tech guys did upstairs, as I could barely remember a thing. A scratch the length of my arm and half as deep as my wrist striped one side, and I couldn't even remember when that had happened. Grabbing the sidestep, I hauled myself beneath my monster, checking for further damage, but fortunately, most of it looked cosmetic.

"You'd think I would have learned not to run into so many things," I joked.

Or could remember what happened to my truck.

My words fell flat in the garage, and when I turned around, I was alone.

The floor to Liam's office was dark, the corridor silent, but light flared from beneath his door. I strode past empty offices and conference rooms, my fist raised but the door opened before I could take my angst out on it.

Liam's face was hidden behind its usual, peaceful mask. He nodded me into his office, his phone pressed to his ear.

I sidestepped him, dwarfed in a largely empty office. All it contained was an enormous desk clean of anything and a bookshelf filled with leatherbound law volumes that looked like they had never been opened. A worn patch of carpet striped the length of the office space. Liam trod the well-worn threads as he spoke softly into his phone.

City lights illuminated the dark city beyond Liam's twenty square feet of peace. He ended the call and turned to me with a raised eyebrow.

"Why is Joey in my other workplace?" I asked, fighting down the urge to shake the silent man. Was this how Danny felt when I didn't respond enough to him? I filed the thought away to consider later.

"Because you're the only one without a vested interest in not immediately giving into the urge to murder him." Liam turned the phone over in his hand once.

"And you want me to babysit him until someone gives into that base urge? They would have a good reason," I said.

After all, the brother of the psycho who had ruined half of Mila's life and nearly a decade of Cal's had also tortured Mila. Black had been her handler for many years, and the man held a grudge in a manner I'd never seen in anyone else. Danny got feisty at the best of times, and even Liam had his reasons for attacking the man.

"I want you to babysit him until Joey gives into the urge to testify against his brother." Liam turned his back on me.

"Why would he do that?" I might have been asking the air for all the response I got from the ex-special ops sniper. My voice strained at the end; as much as I respected Liam, my loyalty lay with Cal and always would.

"Why would anyone testify against a man who threatened him? He's not the man you think he is," Liam said softly, this phone flicking over in his hand again. He pocketed it in a smooth movement.

"But you'd still take a shot at him, despite...whatever you know that the rest of us don't."

Like why you had him released from jail, to begin with.

"I've killed what Logan sent my way before," Liam said dispassionately.

I thought of the night we had cleaned up Selena's townhouse, her still form carried away in an ambulance. "Fair enough."

"Good." Liam turned around, nodding as he settled at his desk and extracted a slimline laptop from his drawer. His head remained down, and I knew I had been dismissed.

For once, my warehouse seemed a little too large. My monster took up a good portion of the bottom floor; a Snap-on tool bench filled every surface and more than half of two walls.

Upstairs held a stainless steel kitchen Danny had helped me install a few years ago when he first joined the task force. The boy weighed in a good deal less than me, though he was far more driven. His channelled energy had wreaked havoc upon his early career days, especially when he hooked up with Cal's ex.

I shook my head, grinning. Putting in the kitchen together had given both of us a place to put our energy. Jimmy had spent a lot of nights on my sofa stretched out after helping rebuild my monster for the umpteenth time — not from damage, but because we kept finding ways to improve her. Jimmy used me as a guinea pig for her early designs when no one else seemed to recognise her brilliance.

That still struck me as unbelievable; how people couldn't value a girl just because of how she looked or the name she chose eluded me. Those things showed who she was, but they had little to do with what defined her inside.

Jimmy was welcome in my home any night, and until today, I'd believed that she knew that. What I hadn't known was how much I would miss her company when she chose to stay away.

Liam had said to take time off. He'd implied he wanted us to babysit Logan's brother, but right now, that seemed like a far call, at least until I got my headspace right.

Which, for me, meant spending time with Jimmy and a whole lotta family.

The girl seemed to want to socialise, and if that meant my mission was to get her away from Joey, then it would be twice the win.

If she'd let me.

"Keep your thoughts off your face," Danny instructed with apparently infinite patience. The incident room grew small, even with fewer people in it than usual. "And your eyes. If your mark can read anything that clashes with your profile cover, you'll be made."

Greg Pearson might not be the sharpest tool in the shed, but he was rough. If he thought I had set him up, I'd likely end up as the next target for whatever new weapon he had scraped off the black market in exchange for favours.

It was what he traded in. After going out on a playdate with the man, I got to see his process first-hand. He exchanged hardware for favours and favours for threats until he achieved whatever goal he had in mind. It took me one shot with the grenade launcher he had acquired for *testing purposes*. After levelling a small and empty shack somewhere in a back-of-beyond weapons testing range, Pearson trusted me.

His captain was still a little leery of me but had given the nod when I'd asked the right questions. Getting them to accept Ally would be the crux of it all.

I nodded at Danny's words, inhaling slowly through my nose as I stared at Ally across the small table. Her boyfriend, Brett, was a cop from a neighbouring narcotics unit. He stood behind her, his arms folded. She gave a half-smile back that could almost have been interpreted as sweet if I hadn't known what sort of fierce woman lay beneath. But that wasn't part of the exercise.

My fist clenched on my knee beneath the table.

"Body language," Brett said softly, and both Ally and I jerked in response.

I groaned, wishing I could drop my head to the desk as Cal had often done, though I expected Danny might actually slap the back of my head if I did that. His patience wasn't infinite.

Ally and I bartered a drug negotiation over the table, and from the looks of it, both of us sucked. Royally.

"I'm not an actor." I stood and stretched my calves. The gym called, and the sooner I got this over with, the faster I could return to doing things I actually enjoyed.

"You've got this, man," Danny said, rubbing his shoulders against the doorway. He nodded to Brett, who took away the fake drug packets and replaced them with an unloaded gun. I peered at it speculatively.

"Do I get to shoot you afterwards?" I asked with no vehemence, though the idea had some minor merit.

"Incentive. Pass this test, she gets firing range practice, and you get to play with a new toy."

Ally snorted, but my lips twitched. "Dangle the carrot, man."

"It's a sniper rifle I wanted to test with Liam. You get first dibs." Danny held my gaze, knowing he had me.

"You're on." I stared at the handgun in No Man's Land between Ally and me, working through everything Danny and Brett had taught us. Combined, they were a formidable team.

Brett nodded, and I fell into the persona Danny had given me, focussing on the goal, and slipped Joey's face over Ally's.

CHAPTER SIX

JIMMY

"I didn't realise you meant for me to go out in the sun," I grumbled from the side seat of Micah's monster. With a functional dash and reduced extras, the cab of his truck contained a basic seat, floor, and steering wheel, and no more.

We were lucky it still had a windshield.

Micah sent me an amused grin. "Are you afraid you'll melt into a puddle?"

"More like dissolve in a disgusting shower of ash," I muttered, wiggling my fingers at him.

Micah laughed outright, his laugh as big as the rest of him. "Thought it might be nice to get away from the garage for a bit," he said lightly.

Too lightly.

"Who are you, and what have you done with my Micah?" I asked suspiciously.

The grin from before grew wider, colour darkening already olive cheeks. Somehow, it made his hotness increase by triple or more.

I might never be in his league, but there was no rule against perving on a friend.

That made me feel like a creeper. I sank deeper into my seat. Micah seemed not to have noticed.

"*Your* Micah?" he asked softly, not turning his attention from the road.

"I'm sure I have some claim on your hours," I mumbled, swinging my hair between us.

Micah huffed a laugh on the other side of the green curtain.

"Claim away, Tink. I missed you while I was working on the monster last night." He changed topics at lightspeed, patting the steering wheel with familiarity.

I swallowed, pressing further back into the seat. My harness hung loosely around my shoulders, though the adjusted seat belt was already set at its smallest setting.

"I can help tonight," I blurted, then closed my eyes. *Over eager, Tink?* The words reverberated around my head in his voice. "I mean, I could help whenever you need."

"There's always something to be worked on. Saw some of your schematics for fuel distribution. What did you have in mind?" He waited for a beat while my throat dried, and I emitted a small croak. "Tink?" His fingers brushed my hair from my face, his knuckles grazing my cheek.

I started, staring up at him with wide eyes. My heart began its familiar race toward the panic button, but it toned down from the terror I usually experienced. This fear had more to do with...rejection?

If Micah had been looking at me, his attention had well returned to the road. The contact was unexpected and a little jarring. At least, that's what I told myself as my heart pounded away within my chest cavity. Hearing him use his nickname for me put me back into a safe space, though.

"Well, I had thought..." I started, my mind forming the concept in three dimensions inside my head, and I worked through each point until Micah pulled up. "Where are we?"

"Mama's. C'mon." Micah grinned again, his shoulders slightly lower than before.

Any guilt I felt at spending time with someone else dissipated — though I shouldn't *have* to feel guilty about having friends. My head said it was healthy to socialise, though the rest of me fought against it, despite knowing it had the right idea.

My stupid heart, tethered to a man who would never see me as more than the geeky girl who improved his truck, had other ideas.

The passenger side door opened. I fumbled with my harness, but before I could push myself from the cab, Micah appeared at my door and lifted me down.

I found myself held to a massive chest, my feet dangling a good few inches from the ground as Micah shut the door. My hands fell on his shoulders by pure reflex — giant shoulders, attached to a giant of a man.

I could barely breathe around him.

"P-put me down," I said firmly, but my stammering attempt at wording made it come out more like a question than I wanted.

"I never get to see you eye-to-eye," Micah mused, still looking down at me.

An odd glimmer lit his eyes. I watched them, mesmerised, then remembered to talk.

Use your words, Jimmy.

"That's because there's a good two-foot difference in height between us." I wiggled a little in his hold, but it wasn't uncomfortable.

In fact, nothing about him was uncomfortable, considering his proximity. It hit me that I wasn't afraid of him.

Is it just him, or everyone? Am I actually normal? Am I safe?

The betraying thoughts slid across my mind, and I remembered being in the crowd of people next to Joey. I'd covered my discomfort with a very fake laugh I was sure he had noted when he'd touched me. The jostling people had set off enough alarms to know that my new normal hadn't been re-established just yet.

But...perhaps it was a start?

Micah's hands fit almost all the way around my rib cage, but they didn't steal my breath. I supposed that to a man with biceps the size of watermelons, I wasn't a particularly heavy lift.

"Are you alright, Tink?" Micah's amused voice broke my reverie.

"Oh!" I drew my eyes from his arms, relocating them to his chest and shoulders, then up to his face.

Heat rose in my cheeks, my embarrassment scalding any peace I'd managed to gain in those few moments. I wriggled in his grasps, trying to reach the floor and realised my legs were wrapped around his waist.

When in all the fresh hells had that happened?

I closed my eyes, unable to face him. "Please put me down."

"You're going to need to unwrap yourself first."

"Okay." I blinked. My feet flexed, but I still didn't move. Something buttery, framed by tomatoes and a hint of garlic swarmed into my brain. "Oh, my God. What is that?"

My feet touched the ground, and I turned to find the source of the ambrosia.

"Good to know my Mama's cooking can get you off me." Micah snorted, his arms folded as he watched me.

Heat flamed my cheeks in response. "A girl can't refuse good food," I protested.

"Mmnm. I'll remember that." He grinned, reaching out toward me.

His fingers closed comfortably around my hand, which looked tiny and ridiculous next to him. Probably not as ridiculous as I looked, being towed around by the sexy behemoth.

Micah led me along a path covered in wisteria and roses to a cottage house that could have been out of a fairy tale. He squeezed down the thin path at the side of the house. A kissing gate separated us from the growing hubbub around the back of the house, and as we walked into the back yard, I realised I might be gate crashing a party.

What looked like hundreds of people milled about a paling-fenced yard. Three long tables laden with platters of Italian food, bread, and drinks fed the horde. I spotted at least two barbeques, the scents of roasting vegetables, fresh pasta, and zesty lemon filling my head.

"Who are all these people?" I asked in half-whisper, slightly stunned at the population that overfilled the area.

"My family." Micah closed the tiny gate behind us.

"All of them?" The stage whisper disappeared, dissolving into full-blown panic. "I don't belong here."

Micah smiled over his shoulder at me, tugging me a little closer. His gaze dropped a little as he tucked me into his side in a one-armed hug. "Better?" He murmured.

Oddly enough, it was. I breathed at a normal rate. "Must be because you make a wall between me and the rest of the world," I gave him a gentle push which, unsurprisingly, did nothing.

"If that's what you need, Tink." His dark eyes promised me he would never fail to be that wall if I allowed it.

Smiling easily for the first time since we had last worked on his truck, just the two of us in his garage, I let him lead me deeper into the yard and through the throngs of people.

My shoulders tried to tense up, but the muscles didn't hold for more than a moment.

"Doing okay?" Micah murmured.

"Actually, yeah," I answered, somewhat shyly.

Until a familiar aroma wafted under my nose.

Before I had thought it through, I stood at one of the tables, peering into a dish. Dark coils of long pasta were studded with tiny scallops and roasted tomatoes, still in their skins.

"That smells so good." I inhaled with a tiny sigh. I didn't even care if anyone listened in. "I haven't had squid ink pasta since–"

I broke off, catching my bottom lip sharply between my teeth. Rolling the soft flesh over sharp teeth had become a bad habit, but the pain drew me back from the brink of memories I couldn't deal with anymore.

"Good thing it's my speciality." A short, rotund woman beamed at me, pulling me into a hug. Which was comfortable because she stood no taller than me.

I inhaled a second time. Home, warmth and... I looked over to Micah. His face cleared of all tension, but his arms hung just out from his body. I smiled at him over her shoulder and was rewarded with a small one in return.

"It's amazing, Mama."

"Ohhh, it's nothing. Just feeding them." She swept out a hand to encompass pretty much everyone crowded into her backyard. Micah's mother was as small as me, but she managed all these people. My head swam with it.

I laughed. "Nothing much, then."

"Not at all. And you brought my boy home." She raised her arms, the epitome of every movie-made stereotype, reaching up to hug Micah.

"Well, he brought me–" I said softly to the air.

Micah looked up with a grin, his arms wrapped around his mother, who didn't look ridiculous next to him.

Not like I must.

Mama caught my hand, introducing me in a whirlwind of cousins upon cousins whose names I promptly forgot. At first, I glanced back at Micah while certain terror covered my face. He just shrugged with his hands in his pockets as if to say *this is how it is.*

After a while, I learned to just let her tow me around. I hoped the tour would finish back at the table so laden with food that brought up pleasant feelings — though I wouldn't go so far as to call them memories.

Finally, she released me back to Micah, my head awhirl with names. He passed me a bowl overflowing with the squid ink spaghetti I had drooled over earlier, tomatoes and a sprig of fresh basil perched on top. He led me to a garden bench, perching on one end.

I stared at it, waiting for the thing to crumple beneath his mass.

"This thing has held up for too many years. It's not going to fail me now." Micah shook his head, laughing. "I've cried on Mama's shoulder over a broken heart when my first boyfriend dumped me and when a girlfriend moved out of state. I was fourteen."

"Ow. That sucks." I dug around in my bowl and extracted a scallop. The buttery seafood dissolved in my mouth, and I let out an appreciative moan.

"That good, huh?" Micah asked.

My eyes popped open. He watched me, slightly hunched over his own bowl, looking no less ridiculous on the bench than I likely did, perched next to him.

"Yeah. That good."

"You've had it before?" A question nestled deep within his probing gaze, but Micah reigned it in before it became too imposing.

"It's Australia. Seafood is our jam." I grinned, thankful for the exit strategy he had given me.

"Too true." A second behemoth plunked down next to me, others following in fast fashion.

I had thought Micah was as huge as any reasonable male could be, but these men put him to shame. Not in the same crafted muscle Micah had amassed over his body. No, these men were just huge all over. The bench seat trembled beneath their combined weight.

Uh—" I made to get up, but a hand shot out, looping around my waist. Hands passed me across several sets of knees before I settled against a warm and comfortable body.

Micah's eyes danced with humour as he balanced me lightly across his legs. His hands barely grazed my skin, the tentative touch letting me know this wasn't a cage I should feel the need to escape from.

But I didn't have the usual urge to flee. Instead, I leaned just as lightly into him. Micah stilled, then his chest vibrated as he laughed at something one of the cousins — I *thought* they were cousins — said. His hands touched my skin fully, and when I didn't jerk or move away, they sank a little deeper.

I followed the conversation with difficulty. Micah's touch proved to be a time-consuming distraction until I concentrated harder and realised the men spoke in at least three different languages I could distinguish. Eventually, I finished my food and leaned back into the wall of muscle behind me.

Safe. An enormous group of people surrounded me, and I hadn't panicked once. Well, I'd had a moment when Mama began to tow me around the yard, but we had only just arrived then. And more than being safe in a group of people, I was safe with *him*.

Crowds were different. You could get lost amongst a collection of bodies, and they offered some degree of social safety. But with Micah, even in full-body contact with him, and I was totally, utterly, safe.

I could have cried.

Instead, I leaned against him, seriously considering a second bowl of the black pasta, wondering how we — *how I* — had gotten to this point without realising it. Was this how people just woke up one day and realised they were in love?

Oh, hell no.

Air jammed in my throat, unable to move in either direction. I began to hyperventilate, doubled over at the waist, attempting to gasp air that didn't seem to come. My lungs burned, but they wouldn't inflate.

Offers of thwacking my back over the Heimlich manoeuvre were debated above me. Only when a hand touched my shoulder, and I flinched violently, did the debate finally end.

Micah rose, lifting me like I was a feather. Which to him, I probably felt like one. I managed to gulp air amidst the tears, and who knew what other bodily fluids covering my face, cowering in his arms.

The hubbub receded behind us, and Micah set my feet gently down on the grass next to his truck. I swiped my sleeve over my eyes, which had to be puffy and red all over. It took several goes to clean my face, and I was positive that combined with my worm-pale skin and green hair, I resembled an out-of-season Christmas disaster.

"No crowds, huh? How are you doing?" Micah checked me over.

"Yeah," I whispered, listless. Every inch of energy zapped from my body in a mass evacuation. It hadn't been the crowd, but I had no intention of sharing with him *why* I had just had a massive panic and choking attack at his family barbeque.

Micah stood silent for a moment while I studied the tops of my boots. His massive hands closed around my waist, and he lifted me up into his truck, buckling the harness around me with care.

"Where do you want me to take you?" he asked, brushing hair back from my face.

"Anywhere," I whispered, staring at my hands, willing the tears not to come.

They did, anyway.

CHAPTER SEVEN

MICAH

Jimmy curled in my passenger seat, staring silently out the window, while I struggled to process what had happened. Something had changed in the restless girl who had settled on my lap, even after she'd been passed over a few cousins. Her body had pressed into mine, mirroring a need for contact I'd only dreamed about. No, it hadn't been the crowd. Whatever had changed in Jimmy had happened inside her own head. I couldn't help her if she wouldn't let me in, but it wasn't my place to pry.

It hadn't been food she had choked on; that much was obvious. I wanted to understand the change in her without doing more damage to her fragile and brittle facade.

You don't know, do you?

Joey's words haunted me on the drive from suburbia across the city, and paired with those dead eyes and little smirk, I wanted to take a page out of Danny's book more than ever.

The criminal genius' little brother seemed to be a chip off the block when it came to mind fucks.

I needed to speak to Liam, but not tonight.

"Mine okay?" I asked lightly.

Jimmy had said she didn't want to go home, and I started to get an inkling of why she never used the word. What I didn't get — and I cursed myself viciously for not asking earlier — was *why*.

She nodded, and I took the exit that would lead us into the bowels of the industrial estate I called home.

The large buildings emptied as dusk fell over bare streets and utilitarian buildings. It stood in a stark and somewhat remote area, well removed from the chatter of the city, but it suited me. Larger spaces meant I had room to think, as well as providing privacy.

I'd never thought to hide away in it, but if Jimmy needed to do that, she was welcome for as long as she wanted to stay.

If she would take the charity. I had a feeling she would consider the offer to be exactly that. My mind ticked over, a plan forming of how I could provide her with a sanctuary without it sounding like pity.

In the back of my mind, a second idea flickered into existence. My conscience battled against it, but I knew I would need the information if I couldn't get Jimmy to share it with me. I stared straight ahead as I turned onto my street, Jimmy still hunched in a corner, turned away from me.

"You know, I would have thought you had enough of Mama's food back at the barbeque," I teased, keeping my tone light.

I didn't get a response.

Jimmy curled beneath a blanket that may as well have been hers; she had slept under it enough times. A dark head protruded from the far end, her green hair glimmering as the image on the TV flashed. A piece of garlic bread disappeared into the blanket.

One of my cousins had rushed out with a bag filled to the brim with aluminium trays before I could pull away from Mama's place. I had thanked him perfunctorily, despite my distraction, but now I was far more grateful.

Cooking would have been a bare minimum effort tonight, and Jimmy loved her food, even if it never seemed to put any weight on her slight frame. I adored her, but I understood a little more about the tiny girl who had been hiding in plain sight in front of me for so long. As she dug into her plate, I was glad to be able to provide something for her, even if it was warmed up leftovers.

"That's because your mother is a goddess in disguise." Jimmy's voice was muffled.

"And you fit right in." I nudged her with my toe.

"Never going to happen," she replied automatically. Her entire blanket went rigid, quite a feat for a piece of well-worn material.

"I dunno, you let a few guys handle you today." I couldn't help the grin that rose on my face.

You let me handle you today.

Touching her had been a gift I hadn't realised I was missing. But I knew the words would get a rise out of her.

"You make it sound like a bad thing," she mumbled through a mouthful of bread.

"Did I?" I stretched my arm across her blanket, leaning my hand along her leg where I expected her shin to be.

The size of her lower leg felt right beneath my hand, even covered by a blanket. Thankfully, I hadn't gone any higher, or I might have earned myself a slap — and I suspected Jimmy would pack a punch. Timid as she appeared, the girl contained a leashed passion. I had seen it enough times in her designs when she worked on a problem for my truck.

"Are you right?" she squeaked in protest. Her leg kicked out the tiniest amount, but she didn't draw away.

I took it as a good sign and left it there. But there were still other things I needed to work out with her before she passed out on me for the night — or more likely, crept out of my house while *I* pretended to sleep and not notice.

Asking about why she slept in the garage wasn't an option. Not only did I not want to upset her, but if I was honest with myself, the real problem lay elsewhere.

Not knowing she slept there bothered me more than I cared to admit, but the problem wasn't Jimmy. My only enemy was my ego. Pride made you fall, but it wouldn't take the brunt of the landing or protect you from the damage and the fall out that came after.

Even so, I couldn't bring myself to say the words.

"What did you actually choke on this afternoon? I know it wasn't food." I chickened out completely.

Jimmy's head rose the tiniest fraction above her blanket, two eyes narrowed as she peered at me. Just as slowly, she descended back into the blanket, my heart lurching along with her.

I'd known something else had panicked her, and she'd just given me enough confirmation to ease the guilt already riding me. Squeezing her leg, I offered her a basket of garlic bread with my other hand.

She took it, and when I expected that to disappear into the blanket too, she surprised me, balancing it on her knees instead.

"Peace offering? I hate answering things." She straightened the tiniest amount, pressing her calves into my hand.

My heart wasn't the only thing that jerked.

"Accepted. Plus, a bribe. I need a lot of work on my monster, and I need to keep her here. You up for a week or more of work? Long hours, shitty pay," I warned.

"Just keep feeding me." Another piece of garlic bread disappeared from the basket.

I grinned, refocusing on the screen, but my attention lay with the girl next to me that I dearly needed to wrap my arms around but couldn't.

A shiny, pearlescent envelope sat in the centre of every desk when I walked into the incident room. Jimmy had already risen and started tinkering when I left a plate of food beside her, where she worked frantically on her laptop. She gave me a harried wave as I left, mumbling her thanks.

Very few people shared my life so closely, but Jimmy had always been there, for the last few years, at least. That didn't feel like an intrusion.

I frowned at the glossy envelope, looking around the office. Cal slumped over a bowl of noodles, Black glaring at him silently from across the room.

"Morning," I sidled between the two silent men who appeared intent on ignoring each other.

"What is it?" Black grunted, unmoving.

I picked up the envelope on my desk, turning it in my hand. A seal in red wax sat slightly off centre at the back. I broke it, sliding out a formal looking invitation.

"You're invited to..." Danny read beside me, focussed on the curly writing that had a distinct touch of Mila's hand.

I struggled through the curlicue, finishing the words. "Congratulations, man."

"Thanks." Cal gave me a happy but weary grin, yawning into the back of his hand.

"I thought Black would be happier." Danny glanced at the dark cop brooding against the far wall in a familiar stance and back to me.

I shrugged. "Can't always make everyone happy."

Though Danny was right, Black *should* have been happier. He had been pushing for Cal to marry Mila ever since they had gotten together, and almost daily since Mila had fallen pregnant, especially with her increasing health issues.

Black leaned his back against the glassed wall of our office, his arms folded, chin tucked down.

"Anyway." Danny moved between the two men, engulfing our boss in a massive, if somewhat awkward, hug. "I'm glad you've set a date." He muttered something else in Cal's ear.

I turned away to give them some degree of privacy.

Black didn't.

The invitation was set on a matching card to the glossy envelope, dated for a weekend only a month away. I blinked. With a family as big as mine, I had a good grasp on just how busy it would be in the lead up to a wedding. With Mila's health issues, and Cal's obvious and growing exhaustion, I could see it becoming a stressful mess.

"Have you been planning this for a while?" Danny beat me to it, talking to the room in general.

"No," Cal answered him from his desk, pushing a hand through his usually short hair. Dark circles were a permanent fixture beneath his eyes.

"And you've got things booked?" Danny glanced at Black, who shook his head.

Cal shrugged, flicking on his computer.

"Why are they rushing?" I turned my back to Cal.

Black lifted his gaze to me and shrugged. "I might have pushed. But he was ready. Just stressed."

I nodded, attempting to keep the frown off my face and doing a shite job of it. "Pleased with yourself?" I couldn't help the barb. Danny was rubbing off on me.

"Not particularly." Black leaned back on the wall, his eyes closed. Tiny lines around his eyes belied the calm he projected. "Both just worried for the girl we love."

"She'll be alright," I patted his shoulder. Black didn't so much as move. "She's got both of you to look after her, and she knows you care."

Danny wandered back to me, pocketing the invitation. "How's Joey going at the track?"

"Have you got a mini-me spy in my garage?"

"Hell, no. Just that nobody else has been bitching about him, and I know you won't, even if he's sleeping in your loft." Danny paused, studying me. "He's not, right?"

"If Joey was in my house, I–" I broke off, pressing my lips together.

Danny raised an eyebrow. "It's fun seeing you pissed off with someone who's not me."

"To be fair, I was never really pissed with you."

"Uh-huh. Gym?" His eyes said everything he couldn't, but Danny was right; the room was getting overcrowded.

"Sure, meet you in the lift." I waited until Danny had left the room and leaned down to speak quietly in Cal's ear.

The workout was overdue and felt good, the rivers of sweat that poured out of my skin even better.

"How long have they been fighting?" Danny spotted me as I pushed the bar. It held far from the most I had lifted, just enough to stretch for the push.

"Since Black's last case. Cal sided with Liam on something. It sort-of broke them." I released the bar to him.

"Black's always been a grumpy asshole." Danny joked, casting a quick look over his shoulder as he put the bar back on the rack.

I straightened, grabbing for a towel. "Keep saying it if you want to get your ass handed to you. Aren't you the king of all things surveillance? Why don't you know what's going on in every room?" I grinned, tossing the towel at him.

Danny caught it by reflex and flung it back at me. "I don't bug *us*, asshole. We're a task force, not a fucking spy school."

"May as well be, with the shit that Liam pulled." I stretched gently, my singlet sticking to me.

Danny watched me. "Are you ready for your meet with Nelson?"

I raised one shoulder. "Should be, seeing as I set it up. Fucking nerve-wracking, to be honest."

"You'll get used to it."

"Piss off. That shit's for crazy bastards like you."

"True that." Danny swiped a hand over his head, slicking it back. "We done?"

"Not quite. I need a favour." The words tasted bitter, but I said them anyway, knowing she would never trust me again if I followed through with this.

"What sort of favour?" Danny squatted, under the pretence of stretching muscles he had already stretched, falling naturally back into the unassuming role that would get him the most information possible.

Not spy school, my ass.

"I want you to do a search. On Jimmy." Her name caught in my throat.

Even Danny's acting skills failed him.

"Hell no, I'm not doing a search on our friend." He rose too fast, wincing, but his gaze stayed hard and steady on me.

"This isn't just curiosity. I can't keep her safe if I don't know her story." I held back, unwilling to admit defeat just yet.

"Whaddya want me to do, dude? Look her up?" Danny raised both hands in a *WTF* gesture. "Because invading her privacy is going to solve everything. Just ask her what you want to know."

What did I want to know? Why she slept on the floor of my garage, why she edged away from me when I'd never seen her get antsy about being near me before, until Joey.

Why she was suddenly comfortable in my arms.

Something about her had changed, and I needed to know she was okay, that somehow, Logan hadn't gotten to her through Joey. I wished like hell that Liam hadn't introduced him to my tiny slice of peace.

I needed to know the changes were really *her*.

Or maybe you just didn't take the time to notice.

My head dropped to my hands, running them through my hair in mimicry of Danny's movement earlier.

Hadn't I? We worked together for nearly eight hours every day. The only people I spent more time with other than her were the people in the office several floors above us.

I rolled my lips between my teeth, running through all the options, but one thing kept jumping out at me.

Why was she spending so much time with Joey, and how long had it been going on? How long had he been free? The questions kept coming until my head filled with them, and I didn't have a single answer.

I nodded into my hands, telling myself that jealousy of sharing a special person in my life with someone who might have the power to rip it all apart had nothing to do with it.

Keeping my voice low, I leaned my elbows on my thighs, running my hands over my head. "Do it. Look her up."

I rose without looking back at my silent best friend and walked out of the gym before my conscience could catch up with me.

Cash scattered across the small tabletop, fluttering dangerously close to the edge. Greg Pearson glanced sideways at me.

"Don't look at him; he's not the boss," Ally snapped, flinging her hair over her shoulder.

I sipped my beer, genuinely ignoring the entire scenario. Ally laid it on thick — a little too thick, for my taste

— and I didn't want to give her away. Fortunately for me, Pearson was a sexist asshole, and I was going to enjoy watching Ally hand his ass to him one day. Hopefully soon.

My phone vibrated in my pocket. I ignored that too, though the urge to continually poke Danny pulsed through my hand. I squeezed the beer can a little too tight, and it crinkled in my hand.

Pearson looked over at me. "Playtime gets a little addictive, huh?" He smiled, the edged curling up into a sneer.

Maybe you'll lose the sneer if I plant my fist in your face.

I was never aggressive like this at work; what the hell was wrong with me? Scratch that — I knew exactly what was wrong with me, and it was missing from my life, right now, sporting a head of mermaid-green hair.

Concentrate, you bastard.

"What she said." I leaned against a brick pillar propping up the range patio, though to call it one was generous.

The building was utilitarian, to say the least, situated in the middle of an open field of a weapons range not currently in use. There was no way in hell anyone was listening in, and Nelson had patted us both down the moment we walked into his meeting. He wasn't stupid, but hopefully, his ego would get in his way.

"Letting your girl do all the work?" Nelson flicked his eyes between us. Ally's back went rigid, and I could have kicked her. Letting these dirty cops know something got to you was a bad idea. Hell, they weren't dirty — they were downright filthy. And if Ally tripped up...

"Sure," I shrugged, sending Pearson an amused glance, "as long as we get the hardware we talked about."

"Got it here." Pearson patted the crate he was perched on.

"Won't your boss twig if you start bringing in a truck's worth of goodies?" Nelson straightened, a speculative gleam in his eyes.

"You mean Cal?" I asked idly, only just beating Ally to it. Her mouth closed hard. She folded her arms across her chest and pretended to glare at me. Okay, maybe more than pretended.

"Liam." The gleam hardened.

Well, that's interesting.

"Who says I'll be bringing it all to work? Playtime's so much more fun." I held Nelson's stare, channelling my inner Danny. Maybe I should join his fan club and get a WWDD bracelet.

Pearson let out a high-pitched giggle.

I raised my eyebrows as I stared at Nelson, who stared right back, but the dog-on-dog routine got tired fast. Ally turned a fascinating shade of red in my peripherals.

Nelson finally twitched, his hand slapping down on the cash covering the table with a crash. Pearson and Ally both jumped. "Call it a down payment. You want it; I need twice as much."

"Did you just make that decision now to prove how much of an asshole you are?" Ally snapped, not entirely out of the character she and Brett had brainstormed up for her.

Nelson never looked at her, and I shook my head.

"Nope, he planned it all along." I gripped Ally's elbow, tugging her around. A gentle squeeze through her white suit jacket brought her potential tirade to a halt. "See you fine gents later. Thanks for the beer." I nodded to Pearson and towed Ally across the paddock.

"Are you fucking mad? We could have had him then," she groused when we were far enough away for her to let loose.

"Nelson never intended for you to get those weapons today. I doubt the crate is full of more than some rocks and a *fuck you* sign. He wanted to test us," I said gently, releasing her arm.

"Fine," Ally grumbled, hoisting herself up into Danny's truck we'd borrowed for the day. He was right; I barely fit into anything else — especially not Ally's new, pristine convertible. "But you get to plan the next set up. I want this over with," she strapped herself in, fussing far more than was necessary.

I started the truck, its gentle rumble giving me a pang as I pulled away from the weapons range.

CHAPTER EIGHT

JIMMY

I pulled the wrench out from where I had managed to jam it somewhere in the engine. It was one of those places that couldn't be accessed either by above or below without becoming an instant contortionist and had to wriggle into some tight spaces just to retrieve the thing.

Rubbing filthy, bruised knuckles, I sat on my ass, the cold cement stealing my warmth and wondered if it wasn't a euphemism for my life to date.

I stared up at the engine suspended above me. It was a spare that Micah happened to have lying around. I shook my head, but a smile crept over my face, anyway, which drove my irritation at myself higher.

"Why did you bring me here, Micah?" I muttered, the tool clattering on the floor. Tiny echoes bounced around and quickly faded in the large, almost overwhelming space.

Unless Micah was in it, of course.

The man filled my life like he filled his warehouse or any room he happened to walk into, regardless of its size.

Technically, he employed me. And in a past life, that might have bothered me.

Micah didn't seem to realise I didn't collect any dollars from the job or that I slept in his garage, usually beneath his desk. Though that might seem a form of torture, it had become ingrained into me from over three years on the streets. Somehow, the sofa he had bought offered little solace. Having a wall to my back felt safer, more protected.

Hidden.

I slumped on the cold concrete, sluicing grimy hands over my hair. My green was beginning to fade, and I'd have to beg a few dollars from someone to recolour it. Keeping up the facade had become my main focus in life. Everything else — working with the trucks, with amazing drivers like Micah, using my skills — came as a massive bonus to a very crippled and stunted life.

A hot shower waited upstairs, fresh food in the kitchen. Lots of food. And despite arguing otherwise, I knew Micah could cook as well as his mother.

I groaned, thinking about my mortifying exit from Mama's house. The older woman had been so kind and beautiful. I would have done almost anything to help her — which had including letting myself be towed around her family. And that brought me straight back to Micah.

And staying in his warehouse all day while he worked, though he had told me himself they had little work to do. He had effectively given me freedom and space under the facade of trust and work. The lines began to meld until I couldn't work out what was real — and what I had blown out of proportion in my own mind.

Distractions had become my key go-to. I had a new open-source graphics program to play with. But redesigning the things in the world I could see errors in was reserved for the quiet hours when everyone else slept, and my mind kept going.

There had been no official diagnosis, but plenty of my teachers through high school and into University had commented on my distracted nature. My choice to drop out broke no expectations, though distraction had very little to do with it.

I tapped my bare toes on the floor, almost numb as I stared at the engine hanging above me. It was held by a few well-placed chains Micah had tossed around a collection of hooks we often used when reconstructing his monster. Usually, after we had deconstructed the thing. But the parts went back together nicely, improved in some fashion or other.

Sighing, I wiped my hands off, sending a quick email from my laptop. Tiny fingerprints covered the keyboard. I swiped my shirt across it, noting the grease stains that covered me and wondered if I should care.

Micah didn't seem to, and neither did Joey.

When a message came back from the wayward boy, I climbed unsteadily to my feet and went to find my boots.

"You've never driven a rally car before?" Joey grinned.

He watched as I ran through everything he had instructed, tapping the handbrake, the gears, the pedals. Finally, I fessed up.

"I can't drive." I stared at the steering wheel, studying the spaces between the arms, shadow and light clashing on the dash beneath.

Joey leaned back, laughing. "Mech-girl. Holy shit."

"What?" I frowned. "It's not that uncommon."

It wasn't that uncommon. Right? I stared back at him in uncertainty.

"I know you can't drive." He tapped the gear shift. "Now, go through it again."

I sighed, recounting every step by rote until I had them all correct. Finally, I got to start the car.

It cranked with a hideous screech.

I withdrew my hands fast enough to smack myself in the face. "It's not meant to make that sound. The monster never sounds like that."

"Well, that's true." Joey wiped his face, tears forming in the corners of his eyes, his shoulders shaking. "But a car is a tiny bit smaller than a monster truck."

I glared at him. "Don't you make fun of me."

"No fun here. None at all." Joey suppressed laughter, though his eyes still sparkled as he held up his hands in mock defence. "Wanna try again, Mech-girl?"

He reached across me, showing me the notches on the ignition, where to turn the key to, so it started but didn't over-crank. I flinched back at his nearness, the tiniest movement.

Joey paused, silence filling the space between us. He continued to instruct me in a soft voice and blessedly didn't try to address the elephant in the room.

It turned out that once I had the basics in practice, driving was nowhere near as hard as I had expected it to be. By the end of the day, Joey had me drifting lightly around the dirt roads. It was nothing as showy as what he had done when we had last driven together, but it was certainly a start.

Shadows stretched across the track when my stomach growled.

"I should get you home, huh." Joey didn't phrase it as a question.

I stared at him. "Why are you funny about taking me home?" The thought that I might have a home, albeit a facade of one, gave me a jolt.

"You know you're welcome at my apartment." He grinned again, but this time it didn't reach his eyes.

"I do know, and thank you, but...I've been working out of Micah's place for years. It's..." *Comfortable. Familiar. Safe.* "It's where half my stuff is, and there's a few partial projects I'm still tinkering with parked around the bottom floor."

"Fair enough." Joey dangled the keys, dropping them. "Wanna drive home?"

I caught them by reflex, shaking my head. "There is no way that would be safe. You're up, Moon Unit."

Joey caught the keys I threw back at him, watching me.

I shrugged, feeling every one of the layers I protected myself with and realised how thin they had become. The tiny pea beneath the layers of mattresses waited for the princess to appear and complain about me. The car door handle warmed under my hand. I yanked it open, sliding into the passenger seat.

Joey started the car, then turned to me with a thoughtful look on his face. "You wanna pick up some..." he gestured at my hair.

"That would be great." I scrunched a handful of straight hair, remembering how faded it had gotten. "Thanks."

Joey dropped me back at the warehouse well before Micah would be home from work. If he wasn't working, he usually hung at the gym with Danny, which could be hours.

I curled up on the sofa in the loft with my laptop perched on my crossed knees, the smallest tray of Mama's leftovers slotted between my legs. I picked at the food as I turned ideas over in my head, tweaking a few newer designs I knew I wouldn't develop much farther without bouncing the idea off Micah. My threadbare rug wrapped tight around my shoulders.

I hated that the back of the sofa faced open air. Micah's bedroom — just a very low bedroll in a Japanese style — sat behind a partial wall. I had never ventured into his space, respecting his privacy as much as he did mine.

Until last night, when he had started asking questions. I'd batted them all away but knew my deflections had far from satisfied him. The reaction was one born of reflex, of ingrained survival instinct.

Micah's questions hadn't bothered me, not to the point of becoming uncomfortable with them for any reason other than embarrassment, and that seemed like a reasonably crappy idea. Resolving to try to answer something with at least a grain of truth, I returned to my drawings, sinking into them until the room faded around me.

The warehouse was dark when the enormous roller door creaked its way up. I fully expected the light to be bright outside and had to check the time — and my laptop battery, which flashed in the endangered species range twice before it sank in.

Micah's monster parked in the space below the loft, the roller door creaked noisily as he locked up after himself.

I placed my feet on the cold floor and yelped. My legs and feet filled with sharp spikes that seemed to protrude from the soles of my feet. I hobbled to the kitchen, attempting to clean up after myself as circulation returned painfully to my limbs.

"Hey, Tink." Micah surprised me with a hug, not bothering to turn on any lights as he climbed the stairs.

To be fair, neither had I. My laptop sat dormant on the coffee table where I'd been sitting since Joey brought me back.

I squeaked as huge, warm arms engulfed me. Wriggling for a second, I fought with my initial panic, mentally reassuring myself that this was a safe place and a safe pair of arms.

A large, muscular pair of arms that didn't appear to have any intention of letting go.

"You can put me down, now." I patted Micah's bicep, astounded at the density of the muscle that covered him. I curled my hand around it and did the same on the other side. My fingers barely reached the halfway mark.

"Nope." Micah lifted me fully off my feet, turning to lean his back to the benchtop. "Not letting you go, Tink."

"Uh-" I released his arms, wiggling to get them inside the circle of his arms, and pressed my hands to his chest so I could look up at him, the little of his face I could see in the darkness. "Is everything okay?"

"Cal is getting married. To Mila," he informed me, as though there had ever been any doubt.

"Congratulations. They deserve it." I said, my heart squeezing a little at the thought.

"I'll pass it on. Didn't think you'd be one for weddings, much."

"Hah. I can see where you might have gotten that impression." I grinned at eyes I couldn't fully see. "But the thought that two people could find each other in the mess of life, and click enough that they feel safe together, for...well, ever... there's something incredible in that," I muttered, looking down at my hands. I traced the curves of muscles of his pecs, fascinated. "How often do you work out for every day?"

Micah huffed a laugh, squeezing his arms around me for a long moment, then he set me back on my feet.

"It's not how long you work out for, Tink. It's how much effort you put into a short period of time."

I tilted my head back, staring into the semi-darkness. "Are you trying to tell me something? Because my brain isn't working well tonight."

"Your brain might be the sexiest thing about you."

"Oh." I was inordinately pleased with the compliment. "Have you eaten?"

"Are you going all domesticated on me? Yes, I've eaten. But give me half an hour, and I'll be hungry. Show me what you've been working on."

"Can I steal your charger? I left mine at the garage."

"You know where to find everything. Gonna shower."

I did know where to find things. Micah had a pile of cords and chargers that had once been strategically placed beneath his sofa. Now they resembled nothing more than a mess of wires, each less distinguishable from the next.

Bending down to floor level, I dug about until I caught some ends. In my mind, I began to map the mess out. Sometimes sight was more of a hindrance than we realised. Colours in a knot of over two dozen mangled cords and chargers meant little. I fidgeted about until first, one end of a charger suitable to what I needed was freed into my hand, then the other. I wound it through the mass, loosening ends until several cords came free.

"Got it!" I sat back on my heels, holding the charger victoriously above my head.

"Awesome." Micah passed my laptop to me, filling the space with trays of food.

"Are you going to eat all of that?" I asked speculatively.

The big man laughed, passing me a reheated tray, and settling back on the sofa. I plugged everything in, scooting backward so we could both see the screen and started to explain my mad mind.

"How is it possible to have finished those trays? They were ginormous." I eyed Micah's bulk. "How many brothers do you have?"

He laughed. "None. I'm an only child, amongst a family of a thousand cousins. Mama adopts everyone she meets. Rather like someone else I know. And you ate more than your share, Tink."

"Yeah, but I had to try to keep up with you."

"It's not a competition. Plus, you'd never win."

"Are you kidding me?" I squawked. "There is no way– well. Maybe." I huffed, shifting against the shape of him. In the last few days, Micah had become far less of the unapproachable mass he had always been to a tactile leaning implement in my life.

"You're not going to out-eat me, Tink." Micah tugged my hair.

Every inch of my body froze, well before my brain could catch up with the knee-jerk reaction. The touch was so familiar, so full of memory, that–

I shot up from the couch. Micah swore as my laptop slid to the floor. I swooped and caught it just before it crashed irreparably into the hard surface, my veins fuelled with adrenaline. I collected everything quickly.

"Is everything unlocked in your truck? I'd like to start putting all this together and see if I can implement it in–"

"Tink. Stop." Micah caught my shoulders, ridiculously outsized in his massive hands. "Just stop. There's nothing to panic about here."

There's nothing to panic about except that I've idolised you and created an image I've fallen in love with when you were my only safe haven.

The thought of my safety net being ripped from beneath me, whether it happened now, and I ran, or later, and still I ran, was too much to bear. I retreated backward to the stairs, not bothering with the facade of taking my laptop with me to work.

CHAPTER NINE

MICAH

I frowned, watching the tiny girl running from my loft. Jimmy shouldn't have felt the need to run from me or feel the need to run at all. I'd planned for this to be her safe space. I'd evidently screwed that up.

Loathe to manhandle her, I called out. "Tink. Stop."

"I really, really, just need to get some things done." She kept backing up.

"Okay." I stopped moving, watching her as she retreated, one foot behind the other.

"Yup. Okay. Good." Jimmy kept walking, closer to the stairs than I suspected she intended.

The moment her heel hit the top step and wobbled, I knew I was right. Light in the room or no, the terror that crossed her face ignited something primal in me. Tink's arms windmilled, her body tilting backward in slow motion.

She curled into my arms and off the top step before I realised I had touched her. My knees hit the floor in a controlled crouch, so I wouldn't jar her further.

Jimmy and contact didn't seem to go well together. I held her firmly but with enough room for her to freeze up and leap free if her reflex kicked in, which I fully expected to happen.

Her tiny face un-scrunched from its squint, and Jimmy stared up at me when the impact she expected never came.

"Thanks," she whispered, her lips barely moving. "I didn't mean to–" she broke off, her lips pressed together.

Large, luminous eyes stared up at me, but not with the fear from a moment before. This time, it was like Jimmy truly saw me for the first time.

My stomach clenched painfully. I hadn't realised I'd been waiting for that reaction from her.

Rising onto the balls of my feet, I leaned back, straightening with her still in my arms. She hadn't run yet, though I prepared myself to put her down when she scrambled away from me with every step I took back toward the sofa.

She watched me the whole time, her limbs soft as she curled into my chest.

"Christ, you're small, Tink." I laughed at the weightlessness of her lithe form.

"I eat as much as I can."

"I've noticed. You're doing well if you can keep up with me." I grinned.

Jimmy rolled her eyes. "Fast metabolism runs in the family."

And she stiffened.

Her gaze held mine but something inside me died a little at the fear and shame in her face.

Trying not to frown, I worked my face into some semblance of smoothness, thanking Danny inside my head. If she saw any judgement from me, I knew I would have lost her.

I lowered us both to the sofa, cradling her and refusing to let the stiff surfboard of a girl in my arms go. Then, I waited.

Bombarding her with questions would only push her further into the tiny shell she hid inside. Green locks, dark in the dusky light, covered half her face. I swept the strands away gently.

"I should go," Jimmy whispered, her voice strained and tense.

"You have always had a place here, and," I raised my voice slightly when she protested, "you'll always have one with me. No expectations. Ever."

Jimmy's protests subsided as she sank into me. The stiffness left her body, and she curled into me. The shudders began as small shakes that quickly turned into full-body shudders as she cried, her tiny frame sinking into my chest where she curled into a ball.

I cradled her against me while she let out every inch of emotion that had been pent up inside, weathering the small tempest balled up in my arms.

The sky lightened in time with Jimmy's snores. She'd cried for longer than I had expected, her lithe body turning boneless against me. Moving her to her usual spot on my sofa was an easy shift. The pillows she favoured were already there and waiting for her. I covered her with her blanket and held her feet over my knees until I needed to get ready to go back into the office.

Liam might have given us a hall pass for the time being, but I needed to work out what to do with Joey — and taking blind orders wasn't something I could accept when I didn't understand his motives. A point of view I suspected he would understand.

I left a note with a large arrow pointing to the fridge propped up by a pair of mechanic's manuals for when she woke and drove quietly out of the building.

For once, I didn't head straight into the gym when I arrived at our office building. Traffic built as I entered the city centre, and the carpark beneath our building was half full, even so early on. But Fridays were often like that: early start, early finish. Liam's silver Audi was parked conspicuously in the centre of a block of six empty spaces.

I parked my monster right next to his tiny coupe and took the elevator to the floor above ours.

Liam's corridor wasn't as quiet as my previous visit. Office doors were shut on either side, a low hum of chatter filling the open hall. I knocked lightly, listening for the muffled recognition on the other side. The call came, and I let myself in.

Liam waved me to his office chair, his phone pressed to his ear again — *was the man ever off it?* —but I ignored the gesture, waiting patiently. His eyes narrowed slightly as I passed him, trying not to listen to his call.

It took me a moment to realise it must be Selena. We all knew he loved her, but for some reason only known to Liam, he wouldn't cross the line with her, though she seemed to live with him half the time. Their relationship was a fifteen-year clusterfuck of therapy from Liam's stint in the middle east as a special ops sniper. He had come back from the desert on his last deployment.

His team hadn't.

I knew guilt still wracked him. For some reason, that seemed to mean that he didn't seem to feel worthy of the pert solicitor's love even as much as he obviously adored Selena. Distancing himself from her did neither of them any favours.

"See you soon," Liam said softly and lowered the phone. He turned to me. "What are you doing here? You're meant to be undercover, even if it is forced." He greeted me in the same breath as he ended the phone call, his fingers flying over the screen as he talked.

"Case is good. We're organising our final meet, and it should close up cleanly. What's your plan with Joey from here?" I dove right in. Small talk and fluff had never been Liam's style.

My job was to work out which angle Liam wanted me to play his cards for him without screwing up his end goal. But for that, I needed more information.

At the moment, I had no idea where those goalposts were.

"He needs someone to keep an eye on him. Cal isn't in the headspace to do that right now." Liam's lips twitched.

I nodded. With the wedding coming up and a baby on the way, Cal had no extra time for jigging around with someone who shouldn't be free.

"Why did you have Joey released?"

Liam paused, putting the phone down. "He got out on bail." His fingers rested on the screen, still.

"Bail was denied," I countered, waiting for him to get to the point.

"His brother's bail was denied." Liam didn't look up at me, still staring at the screen.

It might have been one of the few moments I had seen him stand still for so long.

"Then you posted his bail. Either way, I'm unsure if you want me to befriend him or use him as cannon fodder on the track."

Liam's lips quirked; that last option appeared to be attractive to both of us.

"That might be easier," he nodded, easing himself into his desk chair. "But what I need is to find out what his relationship with his brother is. If he will testify against Logan, then our job is done."

"Wouldn't that be Selena's job?" I frowned, shaking my head when Liam offered me a seat. I wiggled my toes inside my shoes.

"Let's say it's a team effort," Liam said evasively, his hand back on his phone.

"How many lines are you crossing for this? Has Cal's obsession transferred to you?"

"You have what you need." Liam dismissed me a second time.

I nodded, turning on my heel without another word.

When I reached the elevator, I punched the button for the basement. Right now, I needed that workout.

Predictably, Jimmy had eaten half my fridge out. I placed four bags of groceries I had picked up on the way back on the benchtop. She ferreted through them, sorting things into size and colour coded piles before she filed them away in a totally different order.

I watched with amusement, trying to work out her system. Eventually, I gave up.

"How are you choosing what goes where?" I studied a bag of cold fries that shared a shelf in the fridge next to the cheese.

"Order I want to eat them in, versus health benefits." Jimmy emerged from the fridge and passed me the bags back.

"Cheese and chips have health benefits?" I asked as broccoli went to the back of the crisper.

"Mental health." Jimmy shut the door with a bang.

Air evacuated from the room as she stared at me, a hyper-awareness in her eyes.

"Do you want a job?" I asked before she could say anything or run.

Wariness replaced the alarm. "I already have a job."

"But you don't take any money from it to any bank account you own. Well, rarely, unless it's a cash-in-hand job. And," I extended my palms out, fingers spread, "it's to help out a mate. And Mama."

Jimmy frowned, her bottom lip rolling between her teeth. I watched the motion with interest. Reaching back without looking, she extracted a tub of hummus and half a bunch of celery and plopped onto the sofa.

She perched on the edge of the lounge, breaking celery into thin pieces, and passed me a handful. "Eat and talk," she warned, "or you don't get more."

"Cal and Mila are getting married." I paused, waiting for her reaction. I'd broached it briefly the night before, and though her heart-warming answer had surprised me, I wasn't sure how she felt about actually attending one.

Jimmy crunched her celery, staring at me with a nod. "Okay," she said around a mouthful of food, and I thought it a miracle that she managed any sound at all.

Smothering a smile, I passed her the bucket, arming a few pieces of celery for myself. "And it's short notice. Unless it's for work, planning and Cal don't particularly go well together. Black has been pushing him to marry Mila since she fell pregnant, and Cal is shattered. He's getting no sleep. So, I offered Mama to cater for it."

"Okay." More munching though her eyes had narrowed slightly.

"Cal's asked me if I wanted to bring someone with me... as a guest." Damn, I was stumbling over words already. How hard could this be? "I wondered if you might like to help Mama out, too. I'll help with as much as I can, but I need to be there for him. Would you...?"

"Yes!" Jimmy's eyes lit up. The food made it to the table only just before she launched herself at me. "I would love to help! Oh hell, Micah, you scared me! I thought you were asking me to–" The wide eyes shuttered, and she scrambled backward.

But this time, I wasn't having any of it.

"I *am* asking you to his wedding as my date, Tink. I'd love you to be at the ceremony, but I thought you might like to help rather than twiddle your thumbs in a room full of people you don't know for five hours."

I held my breath, waiting for her to object to my plan of potentially making her a working servant, and prayed I hadn't miscalculated.

"I actually had a responsible service of alcohol ticket once, back at Uni, but it would have expired, so I can't serve drinks." Her legs slid over mine, so she straddled me. She twisted the collar of my shirt between her fingers, not looking at me, "but I can help with food service, probably not prep, though. And setting up, taking it down afterwards so they can have the night together. Wo- would that be enough?"

She finally lifted her eyes to meet mine. I smiled, reaching out to tuck her hair behind her ear, my fingers lingering on her cheek. She blinked but didn't pull back. Something warm burrowed in the pit of my belly, growing just a little, its warmth spreading. It took me a moment to recognise it as hope.

"It's a weird way to ask someone out, I know, but—" I broke off as Jimmy leaned forward, only just touching her lips to mine.

I inhaled sharply, unwilling to move or to break the contact, the trust I had worked so hard with her to make. My hands clenched into fists at her sides, lest I gave in to the base urge of crushing her against me.

"Shut up." She sighed softly, leaning back. "And tell me more about what I can be doing instead of pretending to socialise for- did you say five hours?" She sat back, her voice rising a notch.

My hands fit naturally around her waist, settling her against me. Warmth seeped through her clothes. "Yeah, that's why I offered for you to work, instead. Are you okay to help? I don't want to offend the shit out of you."

"Nope." Jimmy leaned backward, arching her spine to grab the celery and hummus. Her shirt rode up a little, and I brushed my thumbs over the soft lines of her stomach. "Stop that. And talk more." She straightened, wiggling her way down on my legs and plunked the bucket between us.

By the time I'd finished talking, the bucket of hummus was half empty. Jimmy grinned at me, nodding, and helped me plan out everything I needed. Light lifted the fear and worry from her face, and though I had an inkling about her past, that part of her history was still muddied for me.

But everything inside me screamed not to ask her and to wait for her to come to me. The patience that I had always prided myself on dropped away, leaving me with a need I couldn't — *wouldn't* — satisfy.

CHAPTER TEN

JIMMY

Weeks passed in a flurry as I worked in Mama's kitchen every day. Micah had laid out a simple set of plans I had quickly seen far too many holes in. His mother shooed him from the room and laid it out like she was preparing to host the Queen. Watching her bustle about, dealing with no less than nine different dishes at a time, I didn't doubt she would be up to the task.

My job on the night of the wedding would be to give directions to guests entering the venue, serve food, and manage the meals with special requirements. After I attended the ceremony, which set off a whole new contingent of butterflies. I couldn't serve alcohol, and I technically couldn't help prepare the food for Cal and Mila's wedding. Still, Mama appeared intent on teaching me every single recipe in her head.

And while my head was usually in a flurry of its own with new ideas popping out and frolicking in a massive rave party that blocked out the world, cooking was...calming. For the first time in too many years to count, my head was quiet.

Not inactive, but the panic, the stress that lived there, on edge every waking moment enough to haunt my few sleeping minutes each night had dulled.

Peaceful.

The more I worked with Mama, the more I liked her, and the more I worked with her, the more I knew about her son. Not from what she told me, but from her actions, the way she cooked. No rush, no stress, and if something went wrong — rare, but it happened — then she calmly took stock of the moment, working through the problem in an instant and replacing it with one that worked.

It occurred to me that this might be the smartest woman I had ever met. Her brain turned at an enormous speed, but she lacked the residual panic that coated my own mind. That gave her a clear head to start with, and I envied it.

"I think we're done." She patted my back, surveying the eighteen tureens of practice food we had created.

"It's magnificent." I stepped back with no small sense of awe to admire the veritable feast. There were plates of pinched pasta, veal scallopini and mushroom sauce, a tall stack of garlic pizzas, and trays of lasagne laid out on a solid wood kitchen island. "This is...incredible. I've learned so much. Thank you."

I had no idea how else to say it and hoped my meagre words were enough.

"You're welcome, Jimmy." She patted me, an arm snaking out to squeeze tight around my shoulders.

My fear of contact had dissipated the night I'd accepted that Micah cared for me, though I suspected it might just be with him. That I'd accepted that I loved him and that he was nothing like anyone else from my prior life. Mama somehow fell into the same category. The tiny woman and I were of a height, and just like I did standing beside Micah, next to Mama, I felt about as tall as an ant.

"Now, what do we do with all of this? Do we freeze it?" I looked longingly at the plates, but even though the place smelled incredible, we had used all the space in the fridge.

Silence fell in the kitchen.

Mama's hand dropped from my shoulder. The tiny woman's mouth opened, and she berated me in the fastest string of Italian I had ever heard and certainly never had aimed at me.

Finally, the tirade stopped, and she turned to me.

"Freeze it," she shook with laughter, bustling about. "We never freeze, Jimmy. We eat, of course." She collected the stack of pizzas, backing up to the double doors which opened to the backyard and tapped it with her heel.

The doors were pulled open simultaneously to expose a group of men, all larger than the next, parked around a long table laid out on the veranda. Micah sat at one corner, an empty chair next to him.

A cheer went up as she pivoted with grace and delivered the pizza tower, flushed with their paise and hugs. She waddled back to me, a broad grin on her face.

"My boys are your practice guests, Jimmy. Service up." She placed a large platter over each palm, showing me how to balance the heavy trays and walk simultaneously.

It only took us three more trips together, and the food moved outside. A hubbub of chatter rose around the table. Mama slapped too many hands to count, though I noticed at least one cousin slipping a piece of pizza from the pile while her back was turned. He gave me a roguish wink. Micah laughed outright until I scurried back to the kitchen, resembling a red and green Christmas bauble.

I placed plates in front of each of the men, leaving Micah until last, a tiny, folded cardboard name place in front of him.

"Crustaceans." I squinted at the tiny, flowing script Mama must have written out. "You're allergic to shellfish?" I asked with surprise, trying to remember what we had eaten over the last month or at any time together.

"Blow up like a raspberry, and it's pretty much a game-ender for me. Vomiting, fluid exchange...all the pretty things." He smiled as Mama dumped a bowl of lemons and a jug of water in front of him. He gestured to them. "That's basic first aid for a person with my allergy. Might save you from a trip to the hospital."

"I had no idea," I murmured as strong hands pushed on my shoulders. I slid into the seat between Micah and one of his mountainous relatives. "I really know nothing about you."

And I want to know more.

Micah gave me a gentle smile and passed me a bowl of black pasta.

I grinned as Mama thumped the table for silence.

"Bon appétit!" she cried.

An echo roused around the group, cutlery clashing on plates, and for a short while, the only sound was the silence of a happy table.

"I am far too full," I groaned, dragging my feet up the stairs to Micah's loft. "How about I pass you these, and I'll just sleep right here. I can't go any further."

Two more trays were piled into my arms. I stared about, but Micah appeared to have vanished, and on a staircase that barely fit his bulk, that was an impressive feat. Arms slipped beneath my legs, hoisting me into the air. I squeaked, my head bouncing gently on Micah's shoulder.

"Are you okay? Got everything?"

"Your man-boob smacked me in the face."

"You get that." He took the few remaining stairs at a run.

I held on for dear life, clutching my trays of food.

Micah lowered me to the ground in his kitchen, holding the door open while I sorted to my heart's content.

I hadn't realised what I missed about having a home. Not the sort filled with a husband or kids, because I had never gotten that far before my life had been interrupted, but the regularity of having some form of organisation in life — a consistent place to sleep.

Even after three years of sleeping at the track, Micah's loft still rated as a temporary fix for me. I just hadn't known where the next step lay, and the safety net anonymity provided held me in place.

Or maybe it was Micah.

"You worked well with Mama today," he commented, leaning back on the door to his small pantry.

"Are you kidding?" I popped back out of the fridge, where I lined lasagne neatly next to tortellini. "Mama is incredible! The brain on that woman. I think I'm in love," I informed him, closing the door.

The tiny light went out. I patted at the walls, looking for the light switch, night blind from staring at the small but bright lights inside the fridge.

A large hand covered both of mine, flattening them against the wall with gentle pressure. Micah's body exuded heat behind me. His breath trailed the line of my arm to my shoulder, then his lips continued the path along my neck.

My whole body tautened, goosebumps popping out on every inch of exposed skin. A soft sigh, barely a whisper of a breath, reached my ears, and I realised it had come from me.

Micah pressed gentle, tiny kisses along my jaw, then back to my ear, tickling the sensitive spot behind it. His giant hands wrapped around mine, curling to draw me away from the wall, back into his body. He curved around me effortlessly, taking up the space I had tried so hard to put between me and the rest of the world.

Tried, but that barrier failed me, crumbling completely as I turned in the circle of his arms.

Deep, dark eyes on my level stared into me. I reached out with tentative fingers, trying to hide the tremble in them as the last of my barriers were swept away.

Micah didn't move, and I knew I would have to be the one who took the plunge. Part of me — a very *big* part — wanted to scramble away from him and out of his home. But the thought of leaving the warmth and safety he offered tethered me to him.

I leaned forward, pressing my lips very lightly against his. Micah didn't move, except for a reflexive squeeze around my waist, his hands almost completely encircling me.

Closing my eyes, I leaned further into him, letting go, and kissed him like I had imagined doing for far too long.

His hands slid up my back, holding me to his chest as he kissed me back. I settled there, on my toes, enjoying the soft kisses he returned. Micah ran his hands over my ass, sliding beneath to lift me easily onto his hips. My back found the wall behind me, my calves wrapping around him to link my ankles together behind his lower back.

Micah deepened the kiss, angling his mouth over mine. Nothing rushed, nothing taken, just a slow torment that melted every inch of me inside. His tongue swept across my lips, sliding inside to explore in a slow dance.

I met his rhythm, my body releasing tension as I sank deeper into his embrace.

"You okay, Tink?" He breathed the words against my mouth, drawing back a fraction to look at me.

I nodded, not trusting anything I said to come out in a sequence, logical or otherwise. Instead, I gave in to the need to touch him. My hands curved around each muscle, barely able to cover them.

Micah's body was a weapon itself. Every inch of him was worked into hard planes that gave him a carved quality. I ran my fingers beneath the neck of his singlet, but I wanted to see all of him. Tracing along the outlined ridges beneath, I reached for the hem of his shirt, tugging it from where my legs wrapped around his waist.

His hand closed tight around my wrist.

I gasped, my eyes flying to his face.

"If you keep going with that little exploration, Tink, I'm not going to want to stop." His eyes searched mine. Micah tipped his head to brush his mouth over my lips, kissing me just enough to turn everything to scalding liquid again. "I don't want to rush you."

He pressed his body fully against mine, and this time, the sound that came from my lips was more a soft cry than a gasp.

Micah's fingers curled around my waist, squeezing. Unwinding my legs from around his body, he lowered me to the floor.

"I don't think you're rushing me," I said, telling myself my knees were only wobbling the smallest amount.

Micah kissed my nose. "It's the *thinking* bit that tells me we need to go slow."

"Fine." My nose wrinkled; I pushed at his chest and achieved absolutely nothing.

A rumble began in his chest as he stepped back. Space grew between us, filling too fast with cool air.

I wanted to launch at him, to latch my arms around him and have him tow me back into his bedroom. I couldn't see anything that intense ending any other way. But my mind whirled with the thought that he had put on the brakes, not me.

My cheeks flushed, glad of the cover the dark room gave me.

"Tink?" As if sensing my embarrassment, his fingers curled beneath my chin, drawing me back to him. His thumb brushed over my cheek, drawing a tight pang in my heart.

I loved this huge lump of a man, and here I was, the first time he had touched me, throwing myself at him.

"I think I need to maybe go h– um, for a walk." I stuffed my hands in my pockets, sidling away from him.

Micah's hand dropped to his side. He didn't move as I backed away, reaching behind me for the railing, this time.

He didn't chase me as I trotted down the stairs, my head swimming with too much emotion. Didn't follow me as I ran down the short hall to his front door. A welcome blast of frigid air met me as I pulled it locked behind me.

I had thrown myself at one of the few friends I had, letting me talk myself into a corner, all the old insults resonating in my head.

Easy. Slut. Whore.

And I resorted to what I did best.

I ran.

"Stupid, stupid, stupid." I paced the industrial area, making it two blocks before the shivers set in.

You should be used to the cold by now.

But it wasn't the cold that brought on the shaking.

When a car pulled up beside me, Joey motioning to me from the driver's side, I didn't ask questions. I just got in, grateful for the silence and company without judgement while my head tried to mend my heart.

Micah's warehouse disappeared into a haze of lights and shadows as Joey pulled away from the curb.

CHAPTER ELEVEN

MICAH

I had expected Jimmy to run at some point; I just hadn't expected it to happen right after I kissed her.

The moment that moved worlds for me had obviously done something similar to her, too, but clearly in a different way.

By the time I made it down the stairs, my mermaid had run over a block. I gripped the brick wall hard enough to crumble the edges between my fingers. A car passed me. I relaxed with effort, fighting for control with the need to do something — anything. For a long moment, I contemplated running after her. Danny would have a great laugh at that — me lumbering along after all the times I had resisted jogging with him.

Chasing her would only drive the panic that seemed to bubble just beneath the surface harder. My chest closed to a suffocating degree, but I held to my choice. I clenched my hands tight, but it didn't stop my feet from travelling a few extra steps toward her.

A revving distracted me, an ancient and battered car flying past me. A single brake light came on as it pulled up beside her.

Everything I had ever wanted to say to her lodged in my throat.

Jimmy didn't hesitate before climbing in, without a single glance back to me.

A wave of uncertainty gripped me as I watched her disappear into the car.

The door closed, the noise reaching me faintly across two blocks, and it hit me.

Jimmy didn't have a phone.

She hadn't called anyone.

The person she knew who had picked her up was waiting for her at my address.

Jimmy had big trust issues. Issues she couldn't work out with me just yet. I didn't know who else she had in her life she might trust unless it was someone from her past.

Or maybe, it was someone from mine.

A yell that never made it to my lips lodged in my throat. The vehicle pulled away before I could get close enough to memorise the plates at the back.

I etched the shape of the car into my head, swearing loudly, but there was no one around to hear me.

"Have you got anything yet?" I paced behind Danny in the small space of the incident room, sunlight peeking between the slats in the office blinds.

Pictures of the Jimmy I knew lined the left-hand screen. A second screen held document after document that flicked over in succession as he discarded each option as part of her past.

"Whoever she used to be, she's gone to a shit ton of effort to hide," Danny muttered. "I wonder..."

"What's she hiding? What the hell did she do that she felt she had to disappear off the face of the earth?" I couldn't reconcile the image of Jimmy doing anything illegal.

Well, much.

The girl had a hell of a brain on her. Perhaps her University days had turned into a push back at the system? She had a rebellious edge which fuelled an inexhaustible source of creativity. But that could just as easily be turned into something detrimental. Crossing lines didn't mean quite the same thing when you were in a room of like-minded people egging each other on.

Mob-mentality.

It sounded uncivilised even to my brain. It brought up images of men wielding pitchforks and burning people at the stake. But beating the system more often than not had had its roots firmly ensconced in education systems.

My mind ran off on a hundred other tangents, each more unlikely than the next.

"It'll be fine. Have patience, padawan." Danny's lip curled, though his eyes never left the screen.

"How do you do this all day?" I grumped, the edge of the desk biting into my ass.

"Just wait, man. Go. Weights it up. I'll call you when I'm done." Danny's voice held a note of irritation I rarely heard aimed at me.

"I'm not going anywhere." I folded my arms over my chest, sitting on the edge of my desk opposite his.

Danny raised his head. "There are five other desks, dude. Go attack one of those. Staring at my computer won't make this go faster." His voice softened a notch as he gave me a half-smile.

"Fine," I grumbled, collecting my things and plunking them down on Black's desk. None of the team would be coming in, so it didn't really matter which workspace I used.

I tapped at files that didn't need to be updated, poked at profiles but with no active case, I technically had nothing to do. Even the weapons case with Nelson and Pearson had stalled. No one was talking to anyone else, and pushing too hard would raise every hackle the dirty captain had.

"Is there somewhere she might go? Somewhere she feels safe?"

Because she didn't feel safe with me, asshole?

I didn't say it, though the words tripped on my teeth in their barrage to get out. I closed my mouth firmly until the moment passed, thinking.

Once, I would have said that Jimmy might return to my place to help me work on the monster, to sleep. I grounded, dropping my head into my hands, letting the weight thud onto the desk. Maybe I should have sat in Cal's seat.

Where would she go? All her patterns were jumbled, and I couldn't work out where she would be except...

"She left her laptop at my place. But I don't think she would return there. Not yet. Maybe in a bit. I have no idea." The surface pressed cool and hard against the back of my hands. Thumping my head repeatedly on it looked like a tempting option.

"Seriously? Man, you are fucked up with this," Danny laughed.

"Asshole," I muttered into my hands.

"Not the only one." My jacket slapped my back, followed by my keys. "She'll be at the track, dude. I'll get you the info. Just...go look after your girl."

My lips switched with denial, but that's what had caused the problems. Denying what either of us felt, where we both felt safe. Home wasn't a place; it was a state of mind. And Jimmy and I had always connected, bouncing off each other like opposite poles of magnets pushing each other away.

Maybe it was time to turn my end around.

Jimmy wasn't at the track. My garage sat empty, and her things were untouched. I pestered Benny and Craig, even going so far as to question the cheerleaders, but no one had seen her.

Extracting myself from the cheerleaders, however, was a problem.

Craig snickered behind a hand that hid absolutely none of the humour in his face as I picked each talon out of my biceps, offering false platitudes as I backed away. Once I'd managed to remove myself to a safe distance, I shoved down the urge to run. It was becoming a bad habit.

"You know they'll leave you alone if you just pick one," Benny said quietly in my ear as I beat a hasty retreat back across the arena to my garage.

"Hell no, I'm not doing that. And once you've done one, they all expect a piece of you. Remember poor Simon?" I snorted, remembering the driver who thought scoring a threesome on his first night boded well for his future at the track.

Little had he known that the next night there would be a lineup, all expecting him to date, wine and dine them at the most expensive restaurants in town.

"That was so bad." Benny shook his head. "Man learned his lesson."

"So much he moved states," I agreed, swiping a hand over my hair. The empty garage mocked me. Where in all the hells had she gone? "You're sure you haven't seen Jimmy?" I asked in a low voice, though the complex had emptied out.

"She hasn't been here since the last charity ride, man. Usually, she sleeps here, but...it's down season. I'm sure she'll be around when you need her. You could check her computer? Maybe she has something on that." Ben gave me a sideways glance and a sympathetic pat on the shoulder, which felt a hell of a lot more judgemental than he likely meant it. His footfalls echoed in the empty garage as he walked back to his own truck, ostensibly to tinker.

It was my own ego that came under fire, after all. Had everyone but me known the girl was homeless and not done anything about it? Not offered her anything?

But she was my mechanic. While she helped everyone else, she hadn't developed relationships with any other person at the track, past her ability to make the trucks function at a much higher level. Her social skills didn't extend past the people she trusted, and if that made it to a handful of people, I knew I was on her list.

By having my own head up my ass, I'd missed something critical — several critical things — about an incredibly important person in my life. I promised myself I would tell her the next time I saw her.

A tiny seed of doubt settled somewhere in the realm of my stomach lining, growing too fast into a fear that consumed me.

What if we couldn't find her, or she ran too far?

I pulled up the back door of the garage, edging my monster inside. My phone had no messages on it, and pestering Danny would achieve little other than pissing him off.

Hours of the day stretched ahead of me. I stood in front of my truck, tapping a wrench against my thigh wondering how I could fill the hours spreading out before me.

Boots scuffed on the cement behind me — cautious, tentative steps that drew my heart onto my throat. I smiled, my death grip on the wrench loosening a little as I turned to face the intruder on my wasted hours.

"I wondered when–" I broke off, the heart that had risen in my throat turning to stone. "What the hell do you want?"

Joey stuffed his hands in his pockets, looking for all the world like an overgrown man-child. In my world, Danny took that trophy. Joey barely got a look in. Any kindness I felt toward him dried up at the thought of him free.

I hoped to the heavens that Liam kept tabs on him. But seeing as Danny hadn't been tasked with that, I had no idea how he would achieve surveillance on a man who shared genes with a murdering terrorist.

That seed of doubt rooted deeper, grappling for purchase.

Classic Wayde Logan, still fucking with us from behind bars.

Joey didn't smile, didn't take another step into the garage. He just stood there, staring at me with those dead eyes.

"Why did Liam release you?" I held the wrench in a loose fingered grip, but I wouldn't need it.

The lanky man snorted. "Do you think he had any choice about it?"

"There's always a choice." I tilted my head, surveying him while I processed his choice of words. It took me a minute, but then I hit on it. "You offered a deal. And you know you have to follow through with it all because if you go back in, your brother will kill you."

"That's about the size of it."

"Shouldn't you be in protective custody or witness protection?" I frowned, wondering again why Joey had been released. Did Liam just want to see what the criminal would do, to give us a reason to arrest the cold-blooded man a second time?

"Wasn't part of the offer." He gave me a sideways grin that I read to mean that Liam didn't give a shit whether the man lived or died. But hadn't he wanted Joey to testify against his brother? What piece of evidence or incriminating factor I was missing?

I stared at the man who seemed intent on integrating himself into my life.

"Right. Have you seen—" I pressed my lips together, cursing myself as a loose-tongued idiot.

Joey raised an eyebrow. "Have I seen...who?" he asked softly.

I stared at him a heartbeat longer. "Jimmy. My mechanic."

"Ahh, green-haired girl. Yeah, she's often around here. Not today, though?"

I ground my teeth that he had been in my space for long enough to have already established what was normal and what was clearly not.

What the fuck are you playing at, Liam?

"That's not what I asked." My voice stayed even. I inhaled a long, slow breath, reading for the man's body language, but he might as well be dead.

Or just well practised at hiding his emotions and intent from the world. A skill gained by osmosis from the brother he professed to hate, no doubt.

"No. It's not." Joey nodded.

Holding my gaze until it was well past the point of being uncomfortable, he turned with the hint of a smile rising in his cheeks and left the track.

I watched him walk away, but he never looked back. I couldn't help but think I was missing a very big puzzle piece with either his brother or Liam's name on it and a much smaller but no less significant piece of a girl with green hair.

CHAPTER TWELVE

JIMMY

I patted the dough gently. Powdered fingers pressed down, my mind beginning to settle as I worked through the recipe. My heart gave random jerks, usually accompanied by an image of Micah, the press of his body against mine.

Running had seemed the right thing to do at the time, but the more I thought about it, I realised I wasn't running from *him*; I was running from myself.

My fear.

My concentration waned, and the soft mixture spread too fast beneath my fingers.

"Not so hard, not so hard, Jimmy," Mama admonished me.

I nodded, raising my hands off the slightly squashed dough, tracing through the recipe with a flour-coated finger.

"Put in the oven for..." I slid the ball into a tray lined with baking paper and transferred the whole lot into the waiting oven Mama had set up for me.

After going through all the wedding preparation twice, we moved onto other standard recipes of Mama's repertoire — her expertise having no end. But her wisdom didn't end with cooking. She had refused to let me call her anything else, refused to let me worry about Micah or fret over the state of our relationship. Instead, I immersed myself into a lifestyle utterly foreign to me yet completely comfortable.

It was almost like having a family again.

The fears, the terror I had cast aside when I'd knocked on her door hit me at ramming speed. I rocked with the impact, slamming the oven door a little too hard.

Mama looked up at me, a speculative glint in her eye. She nudged soap toward me with her elbow. Her hands were as filthy as mine.

"First, we wash up. Then I'll show you some books." She bustled me to the sink.

I let myself be led, the warmth of hope and love surrounding me. It was such an alien feeling that it took me a long moment to recognise it.

Cleaning the surfaces didn't take long. Pots returned into their higgledy-piggledy piles in the cupboards beneath the benches. Though the kitchen was jam-packed with cooking paraphernalia, it wasn't overcrowded.

"Books are good." I eyed the collection of tagged and dog-eared hardcovers that bored the stains and wear from years of use.

"Good." Mama disappeared out of the room while I finished drying up.

She reappeared as I wiped the bench a final time, checking the bread and setting the timer. Motioning me over to the large table in an adjacent dining room, she opened an old photo album that looked like it held the family history.

When the first photos emerged, almost as small as my hand and black and white, I realised it *was* the family history. She flicked through the pages, showing herself growing up as a baby, with parents who had only just emigrated to Australia. The pictures became larger, the pale polaroids faded as she grew, surrounded by a family that increased in magnitude with every page. Finally, a baby cuddled in her arms, and I got my first glimpse of Micah as an infant.

"He's minuscule!" I burst out.

My fingers hovered over a tiny face that held no signs of chubbiness. All babies were chubby, right? Particularly those who grew up to be the massive man that Micah had become.

"Such a tiny baby. Too small, too early. They said he would never live long. I lost others before him and my nephews, well. They lost both their mothers. So in the end, they are all my boys."

I blinked, my eyes filling with unshed tears as she flipped from page to page to display young men growing strong and healthy. At the same time, two members became conspicuously absent from the photos. Micah grew, too, but he always seemed smaller than the rest of his male relatives. These were big men — their gene pool must have had a very specific marker. Even though Micah counted as massive by anyone else's standards, he was easily the smallest of his close family.

"He competed with them," I realised, flicking to a picture that showed him in his early teens, already developing more muscle than most kids his age could boast.

"He grew up too fast," Mama mourned. "But he knows who he is inside, and that makes him comfortable in himself."

Micah smiled in every picture, but as he filled out into the man I knew, his eyes became watchful. That quiet, observing quality I loved, fully developed.

"I wish I had that sort of self-love," I whispered, then clamped my mouth shut. Shaking my head, I pushed back from the table. "The bread should be done."

Mama caught my hand. "You need to like the person you are in order for others to love you too, Jimmy."

My breath caught. I gave her a tight smile, turning back to the oven. The kitchen filled with the scent of freshly baked bread. I inhaled deeply, the natural warmth of it surrounding me like a warm blanket. My mouth watered, and my stomach rumbled right on cue.

I pressed a hand over it. "Oh, no, you have already fed me way too much," I protested, but Mama placed a knife and a knob of butter between two plates with a broad smile.

"I could never feed you too much, Jimmy." She swept over me with a disapproving squint.

Grinning, I served up. There was no malice in her comment, and I knew she had a deep-seated need to feed everything in sight. It appeared to be one of her love languages. The book of the same name had made its way into my jacket, and I had read it while she turned pizza bases out like an army cook.

The melting butter had my stomach growling way too much.

I ate my fill, then thanked her.

"You have a place to sleep, Jimmy?" The disapproval returned, but I knew she only employed it as a facade to cover for her worry.

"I have a place." I thought of my pile of rugs at the garage, of the sofa in Micah's loft, and wondered if I hadn't worn out my welcome in both of my safe spaces. I kept wondering if I was being selfish by coming back to help out for Cal's wedding when I barely knew him. The only member of Micah's team I had met was Danny, a dozen times, maybe. He and Micah had an odd relationship based on their mutual love for their policing careers and fitness.

Thinking back at the pictures of a slightly scrawny Micah compared to the man he had grown to be, their brotherly competition was understandable. A pang hit me. I had no idea what that felt like or even sibling rivalry. Even Mama's kitchen was alien to me, though it grew more familiar with each day.

If I turned up at Micah's door, would he close it in my face? I didn't think so — he would take in every stray and their fleas. I wasn't sure which one of those options I qualified for, though I hoped I hadn't completely ruined our relationship by running away from him.

It had all just been a little too much, too fast...I had pushed, but he had known that I needed more time. He appeared to have even expected it. But I wasn't sure I was ready to go back just yet.

"I'll be fine." I smiled at Mama, and to my surprise, it came out as genuine.

I walked half the distance back to the city. Wandering on my own had always given me time to think, but running had the reverse result on my head. A few hours in Mama's kitchen and the walk put everything back in its place, though the constant chatter of my mind resumed after a brief interlude. I found a train station, thinking of my laptop at Micah's place and when I might retrieve it.

The track was almost empty of people when I climbed through the fence and put my code in. One of the mechanics and another man I couldn't quite see waved when I poked my head out of Micah's empty garage. His truck was gone, but a fresh oil stain coated the floor. He had been here, working, and I had missed him.

My heart divided into two parties as I locked myself into his garage, checking my blankets were still there. It got stupidly cold overnight, and I refused to wake up with a case of hypothermia.

One half of me demanded I use the office phone to contact him. Or at least the old laptop he had stashed away in the back cupboard in the event of an emergency requiring a computer. It had never happened, and I wondered if the thing even had the capability to connect to the internet.

The other half of me wanted to hide away with my own small stash of muesli bars. Suddenly, I was glad I had eaten so much at Mama's house. The walk back had more than worn off any excess energy. My legs ached a little as I curled up on the sofa, fully clothed. Too many years of sleeping on the street had taught me the only time I took off my boots was if I slept in a house. Yet even then, my paranoid brain rebelled at the thought.

Habits might die hard, but fear is eternal, and the need to be prepared still drove my anxiety in every waking moment and some of my sleeping ones. I sank into the pillows, glad of their softness for once, pulling the entire cache of blankets over myself. My eyes were already closing, though the sun would barely be setting outside.

The glow of artificial lights where the boys worked outside the garage filtered beneath the door in a thin line as I sank into a mindless, numb sleep that for once, I didn't have to exhaust myself to achieve.

I was already there.

Icy darkness filled the garage when I woke. I lay still for a long moment, trying to eke out the last remnants of residual body heat from my blankets before it was whisked away by a cold breeze that brushed over my face.

Cold. Breeze.

I rolled too fast onto my belly, the garage swimming as I surveyed the doorway. A shadow filled it. Not Micah, because he took up more space than the actual door. And there was no way *he* could have found me. Not here–

Joey lit his phone enough to illuminate his face.

"Asshole. I was asleep," I grumped, my heart slamming inside my chest. I threw a cushion at him to cover my panic, but the way he looked at me told me he already knew.

I swallowed back more panic.

"You don't need sleep, Mech-girl." He sat in the spot my head had been in a moment ago.

I stared past him to the open garage door infamous for its squeaks. "How did you get that up?" The words tumbled from my lips without any thought whatsoever.

"Really? You need to ask me that?" Joey grinned in the semi-darkness.

My cheeks heated. I slapped him with the nearest pillow.

"Ow." Joey *oofed*, rubbing his shoulder.

"You shouldn't be in here." My fear subsided into a gnawing paranoia, my anxiety fuelling a hundred choices that all ended in doom and destruction. I pushed them all away.

"'Course I should. Anyway, I wanted to see if you were up for a drive. Got a crew going."

I squeezed the undersides of my legs with my hands. "Tell me how you got the door up first without waking me."

Joey held up a piece of wire and a can of spray oil. "Got all the evidence you need, Mech-girl." His voice twisted a little, the inflection giving me pause.

"How did you know I'd come back? Or were you breaking in?" Micah's collection of Snap-on tools were a source of envy and admiration around the track — plus, they were worth a fortune.

"Is this twenty questions? C'mon. I wanna show you something. And the boys pointed me over. They're coming too."

I gave a small nod and let him lead me out of my safety nest, flicking my concerns for Micah to the back of my mind.

The cliff face ended in a pool of water that cascaded down in a long stream from above. The drive out of the city had been a mostly silent one. Joey played music, but I had barely listened to it. An old hoodie that smelled alien settled on my knees as I belted myself in. I nodded, grateful but a little scared of how much I accepted from him.

Micah never asked you for anything.

No, I'd just given him my heart.

I played with the soft fabric as Joey headed out of the city. Headlights stayed behind us as the city receded, and I remembered him mentioning some of the boys from the track.

A quick walk brought us to the top of the cliffs. Joey's hand brushed mine once. My instant recoil returned as a reflex, albeit an unreliable one. Would the urge stay with me perpetually? Wrapping my arms around myself, I stepped back behind him, letting him have the track beneath the pretence of wrapping my arms around myself.

"You don't know what cold means yet, Mech-girl." He sent me an easy grin over his shoulder.

I didn't bother trying to correct him of an utter mistruth.

Craig and Benny cheered behind me, sending an ominous feeling to the pit of my stomach. Ty the Pyro loped ahead on his own.

What the hell had I gotten myself into?

Craig and Benny passed us at the end of the trail. Clothes went sailing through the air as their pale, naked asses dashed forward and disappeared into the darkness.

"Adrenaline Knights!" someone yelled, followed by a splash.

"Our turn." Joey headed toward where the blackness became unfathomable. Yells came from below us. Well below us.

"I'll stay up here and guard the clothes." I backed up from the edge, planting my rear firmly on a nearby boulder.

Joey looked down at me, the bright night casting deep hollows over the angular planes of his face. "You've got this. Pushing a few limits never hurt anyone. And they're alive," he said in a totally reasonable tone, gesturing at the rowdy crowd cavorting about below, their splashes and shouts echoing around the gorge.

"It could be lots of pain?" I offered weakly, folding my arms. "I'm not jumping off that."

"No?" Joey sat beside me, pushing back onto his hands, so his arm brushed by me.

"Nope." I gritted my teeth at the contact; I just wasn't ready for it yet. My chest thumped traitorously, and I ached for Micah's warmth.

Joey stared out over the cliff face. "You know, I met this girl recently. Seemed to me like she had nothing holding her back. Luckiest girl in the world. Free to choose what she liked, free to live." His head turned, his lips curling with the barest hint of a smile.

"Lucky girl," I muttered, wrapping my hands around myself a little tighter, though he had found the chink in my armour. Why run if I didn't survive?

"Live, Mech-girl." Joey stripped off his shirt and jeans, down to his boxer shorts, and held out a hand.

I tried not to stare at the lean muscle thrown into sharp relief. Tattoos interrupted by pale slices of puckered and smooth skin where they shouldn't be glowed and shifted beneath the moonlight, displaying a scarred man who *survived*.

He looked deadly.

Warring sympathy I knew he wouldn't accept collided with a need to know how he had come out the other side of his trials. But his experience was so far outside my own, stunted frame of reference — the homeless mechanic who ran from the wrong people and stayed with the ones she shouldn't. Everything sensible about me was broken.

I had to learn to *trust*.

Making a rash decision that had never served me well, either, I mirrored Joey's actions, tugging off the hoodie he had provided, my tee and cargos. I kicked my boots next to my pile of clothing and prayed I wouldn't come back to find a snake sleeping in them.

Joey's gaze traced over my body, every scrawny inch, taking in the shadows of old scars that would have matched his own in their prime. He gave a satisfied nod, walking backward to the edge, his hand still extended.

"Together?" he asked, a knowing look on his face.

He dropped his hand as I walked past him and out into the open air.

CHAPTER THIRTEEN

MICAH

A Jimmy-shaped lump curled into a ball on the sofa in the garage, her retro boots lined neatly by the end of the garage. I watched the blanket rise and fall in the dim light, leaving the back door open. No one else was around to bother us, and I needed to know that she was safe — more than just seeing the girl sleeping where she had been for the last few years.

Not willing to wake her when she had obviously needed the sleep, I left the lights off. Finding a comfortable spot against the wall where she would see me if she did wake, I slipped my phone on charge, flicking through the information Danny had finally sent through.

There was a good reason that Tink had been difficult to find.

Jimmy hadn't resulted in any answers, nor any other variations of her name. Unsurprising, as we had all expected it to be an alias, for whatever reason. It hadn't mattered when we weren't looking for her. But when Danny had tried to find her, the searches went on and on, yielding nothing. Finally, in a bout of desperation, he suggested checking through the laptop she had left in the loft. If we could salvage purchase details or anything, it might give him the *ah-ha* moment he needed.

But Tink just didn't exist.

The lines of loyalty and morality blurred in my head as I scrolled through the results, fear and disgust weighing them down. The girl on the screen looked nothing like the girl I knew. Three years on the streets had changed her significantly, but desperation could do that to a person.

The breakthrough came with the laptop, but not from the source that Danny had expected. The link to her prior life came via an old, mangled sticker on the base Jimmy had probably stuck there when she ran out of space on the top. Or possibly, to hide it. Together, Danny and I had managed to perform a technical operation in removing the top half of the sticker to reveal the website to a domestic violence centre.

It hadn't taken long after we had found her former counsellor to get the information required, under the guise of requiring it for an investigation.

The counsellor hadn't bothered asking to view the warrant.

Guilt swarmed me, but Jimmy had been hiding for a reason. If the woman she had trusted gave out her information willy-nilly, then I didn't doubt the effectiveness — and necessity — of her concealment tactics.

I glanced over at the body covered in blankets on my sofa. Green hair covered an angular face and a half-starved body Mama had been trying to feed up. When I had been unable to find Jimmy, I'd retraced each step until I found someone who had seen her.

Mama hadn't held back on berating me for not looking after the girl I was certain she had adopted as one of her own children.

But the girl in my garage looked nothing like the girl in the photo on my screen.

The same brown eyes, but rounded cheekbones, and a full face beneath long brown hair curled in a similar style to Selena's made her unrecognisable.

Then there were the bruises.

Rage I had belted down in my teens raised an ugly head. The purples around that full face and gorgeous cheekbones only covered the yellows of previous assaults. No one knew just how long it had been going on because Jimmy ran before anyone could ask her.

Jimmy had changed just enough aspects to effectively hide from any facial recognition software. That is if anyone was looking for her.

And as far as Danny and I could tell, they weren't.

Once upon a time, Jimmy had been born Sally Lockwood. A major in chemical engineering who had changed her focus to mechanical in her second year. Not because of the courses — her grades were exceptional, which came as no surprise. A Dean's Commendation was included in her academic transcript, but it had never been accepted.

By the time it was ready to be presented, she had run and never completed her degree.

The lack of a piece of paper meant nothing to me. But the name on the bottom of the commendation did. She had been recommended by her professor. One Eric Jorgensen. A pale, skinny man with a tendency toward albinism and a glowing alumni record that barely hid the list of accusations buried beneath it. Sally — Tink's — name sat near the top. When the investigation had begun, she had run, and the case went no further.

No parent pushed forward on it. No friend had lodged a missing person's report.

Which meant they either knew and were scared.

Or they just didn't care.

The rage built in my stomach, but there was nowhere to put it. Jorgensen had died a rather horrible death in a rural hospital of a genetic lung disease.

So there was no one looking for her. No one *hunting* her.

My Tink was safe.

And I couldn't tell her.

Whatever tentative bonds we might still have were nowhere near strong enough to tell her about the massive breach of privacy I'd committed while searching for her.

But, looking at her sleeping form on my sofa, I let the doubt that grew in my chest ease into a degree of hope.

"If he slaps my ass, I'm not holding back from punching him," Ally growled about as viciously as a kitten. "And you're not to stop me," she added fiercely.

"Wouldn't dream of it. But Danny's the best coach for that. Plus, Nelson deserves it. Probably Pearson, too. Stop playing with that." I nudged her with my elbow. My words echoed around the empty space.

The unused room situated on the ground floor of an office block occasionally used for surveillance practice was perfect for Nelson and Pearson's needs — and ours.

Ally's pocketed her phone, glaring at me. "I'm waiting for an email," she snapped as she fell back into character, her eyes flicking once to my side. Her phone held the app that would record the conversation. More than that, it transmitted the entire conversation live to where Danny and Cal waited to help us if the arrest got out of hand.

"Can it not wait?" I yawned lazily, not bothering to cover my mouth. "Your social life is fucking with my work life." I gave her the shadow of a grin, grateful for her earlier warning.

"Who has a work-life?" Pearson bumped fists with me.

"Clearly not you," Ally's grumble came out loud and clear. "Are we doing it this time, or are you wasting more of my time?"

"Don't you mean his time, love?" Nelson hauled a black, heavy-duty plastic case between us.

"I don't give a flying fuck about wasting his time," Ally flicked her hair over her shoulder, her words tinged with truth.

"Gee, thanks," I grimaced, knowing she likely *was* telling the truth and turned to Nelson. "How about not screwing with my schedule?"

"Since when do you worry about time?" Pearson grinned, but it was strained at the corners.

Damnit.

"Since I have the cutest little mermaid waiting in my apartment when I get back." I held his stare, then Nelson's. The captain gave in first.

"Cash?" he muttered.

Ally slipped a bundle of notes contained in a rubber band on the table, running her fingers through them. "I thought you'd be clever enough to ask for a transfer to an untraceable account," she said sweetly.

"Everything's traceable," Nelson grunted. He patted the case, but his eyes lit oddly. "All yours."

Ally reached out, but I pushed her hands aside. "Not your job, girl," I put as much animosity in my warning, hoping she would get the point.

I felt Nelson's eyes on me, but when I went to raise the case, a hand slapped down over mine.

"Forgot to disarm it," Pearson laughed.

I laughed too and managed to catch Ally's eyes widening before she swung her hair forward, pulling out her phone to play with it.

The lid flicked open to expose hardware that shouldn't have been for sale in the state, let alone Nelson's area, as she hit send on her message to Cal.

Her gun was drawn and lined on Pearson before I secured handcuffs on Nelson's wrists. When Danny and Cal sauntered into the warehouse, Nelson had run out of insults, and Pearson had a small fist-sized bruise over his jaw.

To be fair, it was a good punch.

"Did you manage to drive your monster in here and pull her apart while I was asleep?" Jimmy sat with blankets pooling around her waist.

"No. *You* managed to sleep through me driving my truck in here." I grinned, hoping it hid the panic growing behind my eyes. I hefted a small bag to shoulder height. "I've been trying to find you to return this for three days."

Three days of utter terror and panic while I tried to work out where she had gone and if I would ever see her again. Had realised how much I loved the girl in front of me. Jimmy — Sally — Tink. Her name didn't matter.

The girl did.

I kept the grin on my face, but it strained at the edges. I hoped she didn't notice. I'd painstakingly glued the sticker back down, Danny going so far as to shade in the edges with graphite to cover our asses.

"My computer!" Jimmy leapt from the sofa, tugging the bag from my fingers. "Thank you. You have no idea how crazy my head is right now." She tugged at the zipper, checking her equipment.

"Actually, I do." I took a step closer, brushing my fingers over the back of her hand. Jimmy froze, staring at me with wide eyes. I closed my hand very loosely around hers, giving her plenty of time to pull away. "My head hasn't been a good place to be, either."

I refrained from saying she had driven me crazy — from what I'd read of her file, she wouldn't appreciate hearing it from me or from anyone else at all.

"I can go," she whispered, blinking rapidly.

I laughed, but it came out harsh, even to me. "Not like that." I tugged her closer, stroking the backs of my knuckles over her cheek. "I panicked, thinking something had happened to you and that I'd never see you again. I missed you, Tink."

Her rigid stance softened, and she leaned towards me, just the tiniest bit.

"Running away is my fall back. I want to stay, but I get sc– claustrophobic." She covered her slip.

"I'd rather have you as my friend than lose you." It tore my chest to say it, but it was the truth. I wanted to be that much closer to her, but I needed to offer her more than cold nights on my couch at home. "But that's your choice. I'm here, either way."

Jimmy took a single step forward, shortening the space between us. "If I want to pick up where we left off?" She looked up at me, completely trusting and opening herself up to a world of hurt.

I swallowed hard, guilt coating me in a layer of grease I doubted would ever wash off.

"You mean running away from me?" I grinned to soften my words, looping my arm around her waist to pull her toward me very slowly.

She didn't answer, rising up onto her toes, her head tilted back. I groaned, covering her mouth with mine. Every fear, every moment of panic, went into that kiss. What I'd intended to be soft and sweet, something safe, transformed into something dark, everything I'd held in refusing to be kept at bay any longer.

Lifting her against me, I lowered both of us to the sofa, catching my hands behind her knees, so she straddled me. I managed to keep my hands light at her waist, though I wanted to crush her against me. Too scared to hurt her, either physically or emotionally. Both states seemed as fragile as the other.

"Stop treating me like glass," Jimmy mumbled against my mouth. "I'm not going to break."

"I'm really not convinced of that." I tugged the hem of her shirt up just enough to slide my hands beneath it, warming her cool skin.

Her hands pressed to my shoulders, Jimmy wriggled on my lap, sliding her knees deeper around my hips. The centre of her contacted me, and even through two pairs of jeans, it was enough to feel her heat.

She gave a tiny moan, her eyes flying open as she stared at me.

"Christ, Tink," I groaned, my fingers digging into her back. "This was meant to be sweet."

"Then be sweet." Her eyes laughed at me, but I heard the challenge in her voice.

I drew my hands from her waist, the shape of her burned into my palms. Jimmy mewled when I broke the kiss, sliding my hands beneath her hair to cup the back of her head. Cradling her gently against me, I lowered my mouth to hers. Every movement was gentle, calculated.

Tilting her head slowly, I angled my mouth over hers, deepening the kiss until she moaned softly, her hips rolling against mine. I caught her hip with one hand, stilling her.

"Sweet, Tink. Remember? You asked for this." I didn't give her a chance to sass me, curving around her to kiss her, our tongues tangling in a slow, gentle dance. The taste of her had me on edge. The pressure of her body against mine did little to satisfy the craving for her.

Sweet, my ass.

Jimmy's hands found my wrists, stroking upward to my shoulders. She traced the lines of my face, tangling in my hair as she settled against me.

"What if I changed my mind?" she asked, drawing back. Her chest rose and fell in fast short breaths.

"Nu-uh." I traced my thumbs down the sizes of her breasts, watching her eyes widen, how her breath hitched.

"Yes." She pushed down onto me, beginning to roll her hips again.

"Remember what you asked for." I grinned against her mouth, holding her to me as I rolled onto my back on the sofa, hooking my legs over the arm of the lounge.

Jimmy clung to my shirt, squeaking.

"I thought you might want me under you," she said, hesitant. Propping her elbows on my shoulders, she leaned up to kiss me, her cheeks flaming.

I brushed the hair back from her face. "You're so tiny."

"I'm not going to break, Micah." Jimmy curved her legs over my hips, straddling me.

"You might," I managed through gritted teeth as she wriggled back to the spot she'd found before. Her hips rolled against the hard ridge of my cock, straining painfully against the denim of my jeans.

Her hands caught mine, placing them over her hips. "Show me," she whispered.

So I did, working with her to find a rhythm that brought a flush to her cheeks. Every inch of determination held me still beneath her. Her tiny body undulated in sinuous movements that drove me crazy, and her knowing smile told me she knew exactly what she was doing.

I let her play and explore in her own way, knowing that my control would be pushed to its limits but having her back, her body contacting mine, was everything I needed.

CHAPTER FOURTEEN

JIMMY

Micah's desire surprised me almost as much as his acceptance of me after I had run from him. But the big man was a giant marshmallow; all love and giving and walking away from him gave me a sense of loss like nothing else in my very restricted world.

The forgiveness in the man was extreme. He refused to let me sleep anywhere but his bed, wrapping his arms around me each night. Though we both stayed fully clothed, I developed a habit of leaving my boots at his bedroom door.

The wedding came up much too fast. I watched him count out plates in Mama's kitchen while I ticked off the supplies Cal and a very grumpy Theodore Black delivered to the house.

Cal and his ex-partner left the house, still bitching at each other.

"Maybe they should be the ones getting married. Are they always like that?" I whispered under my breath.

Micah's laugh turned both Cal and Black back to us, identical, harassed expressions on their faces.

"Do you have to be so loud?" I hid a blazing face behind my clipboard. "Everything about you is massive."

Micah said nothing, only raising an eyebrow.

I flushed hot enough to be a small comet and left the room to find boxes to count.

Preparations for the wedding went smoothly, and all too soon, I exchanged my clipboard for a long black skirt Mama tailored to fit me that I suspected might have fit a tall child. A white shirt appeared, too, though I noted the black, shimmery corset laid out beside it. Shaking my head, I fit it over the shirt.

The laces rose too high at the back for me to do upon my own. Brushing my hair quickly and adding a few light touches of makeup Laura provided, I stared at the woman in the mirror with some small degree of shock. Mirrors were rare in my life, but even I could tell the rounded cheeks and healthy pale pink I'd always been were a far cry from the scrawny girl with hollowed cheeks.

Several cousins had been asked to serve alongside Mama and me. Being useful pleased me, gave my anxious mind something to focus on. There were so many things to get to the venue, and we only had a short space of a few hours to do it all in. Which meant we might be late to the ceremony.

Not really being a friend of either the bride or the groom, this didn't bother me, but it *had* bothered Micah. He had apologised profusely and attempted to get Mama to release me from my duties. Both of us had waved him away, and he retreated with poor grace.

Still fiddling with the ribbons at the back of the corset, I poked my head out the door of the spare room I had been given to get ready in. A large body wandered down the shadowy hall in a suit, his back to me. One of the cousins? I went to bite my lip, remembered the shiny lip gloss I'd applied, and trotted down the hall after him.

"Excuse me, would you mind—" My mouth dried as the man turned around.

Micah's dark, wavy hair was combed back from his face, the small beard he had begun to grow in the last few weeks neatly trimmed. Gone was the cop in the black tee or the gym junkie in his singlet. The deep charcoal suit made him look taller, somehow, though he would likely still dwarf everyone at the wedding.

"Would I mind what, Tink?" he asked, his eyes lighting when he spotted me.

"I just needed—" mumbling and tripping over my own tongue, I gestured to the corset, turning around.

"Ah. Let's see. Sorry if I do this too tight," he apologised, tugging at the laces. He tested the top and bottom ones, working his way along the row.

"No such thing as too tight." I laughed as he tugged tentatively at the ribbons.

"You say that now," he muttered. A few more jerks, and then a click followed.

"What are you doing– oh." I glanced over my shoulder to see him taking a photo.

He passed me the phone. "Am I doing this right?"

I studied the picture. He actually *had* managed to do a reasonably good job — there were a few places that didn't quite line up. I pointed them out, and he fixed them quickly.

"Thank you," I said shyly, running my hands over my waist. Already trim, the material fit firmly around my waist, giving me curves where a few minutes ago I swore I had none.

"You look beautiful," Micah murmured, leaning forward to brush his lips over my cheek.

My skin erupted in goosebumps, and I was glad of the long sleeves.

"So do you." I wracked my brain for a better word, but it had gone on siesta, bringing nothing helpful to mind.

Micah dug in his pocket, motioning for me to turn around again. I frowned but did what he asked. His knuckles brushed my neck, tracing over my collarbone. His fingers lingered there long enough for him to lean down to kiss me again, then he stepped back.

My hands flew automatically to where his had been a moment before. A tiny, metal shape sat in the open space of my shirt. I lifted it, tracing over the curves of the bird.

"It's a bowerbird. They're incredibly hard workers, and they collect things they like."

I studied the pendant, the silver bird with its perfectly shaped, sapphire-blue eyes. "It's beautiful, thank you. But I don't collect anything."

"You collect people all around you. You just don't see it." Micah smiled softly at me, his fingers grazing mine. His pocket buzzed, and he swore quietly, checking his phone. "I'll see you there?" He searched my eyes.

A pang struck me that I could cause this incredible, calm man stress or panic that I might not be there when he looked for me.

"I'll be there. I promise." I squeezed his fingers.

Micah hesitated a moment longer, then he was gone.

Micah stood with his team beneath a gazebo covered with wisteria. Tall Norfolk Island Pines created shade around the park, their dark green contrasting with the lush grass. Cal was tall, looking as classy as I would have imagined from Micah's discussions of his work over the years. Liam looked like an older version of him. I would have thought they were brothers, going by their looks and their hugs from the short man seated beside me who was introduced to me as Liam's father.

Mama sat on the other side of me, clutching my hand, an embroidered handkerchief in her other hand. Micah caught my eye, grinning. Danny said something in his ear, and they both laughed. Micah stopped when a well-aimed elbow from Black connected with his ribs.

I snuffed out a laugh behind my hand as the lot of them broke up, leaving Cal looking very confused.

Music started, and the boys straightened. Heads turned to look along the aisle. A girl skipped between the rows of chairs, scattering petals and glitter everywhere. She reached a woman with short blonde hair who hugged her, covering them both in pink sparkles. The girl headed up to the boys, coating them liberally with pink and purple glitter that sparkled merrily in the sunlight.

Laughter filled the air. Cal hugged her, and the girl went to sit with the woman she had hugged before. Laura and Selena glided toward the boys, lilies and orchids complementing navy, shimmering dresses. They looked so beautiful; I just stared with my mouth open. I was looking

151

toward the boys when Mila appeared, but I didn't turn to watch her; my eyes were glued to Cal's face. His cheeks reddened, his eyes glassy as he stared over everyone's heads.

There was so much depth in his gaze that my heart moved, and I had only met the man for a few minutes half an hour earlier. He watched as Mila passed us in a pale blue gown that emphasised her bump beautifully. My own throat tightened at the love between them, and my gaze shifted to Micah.

He wasn't watching Cal or Mila at all; he was watching me.

And the faint smile that felt like a private conversation between us despite the distance and the other people in the room closed my chest right up.

For once, I didn't run.

Cal and Mila posed for photos signing their marriage certificate, and the crowd broke up, socialising. Liam's dad wandered off, and Micah took Mama and on a walk around the park. Danny collected Laura and followed us.

"How are you going?" Micah asked softly while Mama berated Laura for not eating enough. Danny seemed to find it amusing until she turned on him for *not* feeding Laura sufficiently.

I smiled. "Not as bad as I thought I might. Thank you for pushing me off the edge." I slid my hand through the arm he offered, the feeling both alien and right at the same time.

"I'd be lonely without you here." He drew me closer to him as we circled around the back of the wedding party.

"Really?" I asked, stopping to look up at him. "I—you—" my words stumbled over each other.

"You didn't think I had a heart?"

"No! You've got the biggest heart of any man I know. You look after everyone," I swept an arm out, to encompass the entire flock of people, but mainly aiming for the boys he worked with, "and I don't think you know you do it. I just didn't expect that to ever include me," I finished, somewhat lamely.

Micah looked down at me with glowing eyes that drew me into him. He pressed his hand between my shoulder blades, propelling me forward into him.

"Fuck," Danny swore viciously from behind us.

I swivelled as Mama berated him for swearing, but he waved her down. Micah startled everyone when he swore, echoing Danny, and Mama repeated the process. But before she had finished, the boys took off toward the car park.

Laura looked at me, shaking her head, but I caught a flash of red hair and had a sudden idea what was happening.

"I'll be right back," I called, running after the boys.

A waiter holding a tray of glasses filled to the brim with champagne passed me. I liberated the tray on the way through, praising Mama's training in my head.

Danny and Micah were already herding the redhead off. By the look of her struggling and balance, she might already have had too much alcohol.

"No, I need to get to Cal and tell him not to—" the woman started.

Micah barred her way, and when she raked out at him with a set of sharp, fake talons, Danny caught her wrist.

"You can't do this, Mandy. You need to go home," he said softly with a degree of sympathy, confirming my suspicions.

Cal's ex had been the topic of many garage conversations between the boys, and with all the shit she had pulled over the years, it came as no surprise she would turn up at his wedding. And it looked like at least Danny had been prepared for the occasion.

He slid his phone out of his pocket. "Who can I call for you?" He didn't look at her, but the boys formed an impenetrable wall between the ex and the groom. Well, more than one ex, but I knew Danny only wanted Laura, now.

"I'm not going." Her fake pout pushed out mulishly. If she meant it to be sexy, she missed the mark by a mile.

I slipped around Micah. "Ma'am?" I asked politely, proffering the tray, glad of the monotone outfit that allowed me to blend in with the staff, "can I help you out to the ladies room or get you an Uber?"

Mandy stared at me for a long moment, and I thought I would end up wearing the tray. She glanced between Danny and Micah, and her shoulders drooped. Suddenly looking tired, she took two glasses from the tray and nodded. Mandy looked down in time for the boys to miss it, but I saw the tiny tear track along her cheek and drop into her champagne.

I handed the tray backward, and one of the boys took it; I wasn't sure who. Micah's hand squeezed my shoulder as I led the broken-hearted woman across the park to the reception centre to find some way to get her home.

Nearly one hundred people packed the reception venue, round tables set out in strategic positions to give the best view of the bridal table. I stared at the gathered crowd in something like awe. At the same time, Mama grumbled under her breath about not being able to organise a proper event.

"What's not right about the event?" I whispered to the nearest cousin.

He laughed, passing me a tray full of plates. I hadn't managed to pull off carrying more than three plates at a time, despite practising.

"She doesn't like the size of the wedding." He grinned at me.

"Too big?" I frowned.

He laughed again. "Nah. Too small. To Mama, a wedding is all your family, even the ones you don't see too often." He grabbed a tray of his own, striding across the floor to deliver entrees.

Joey grinned at me as he passed more plates out of the servery. I waved, glad he had fit in.

Liam had added him to Mama's army of waiters and bartenders just before we started our preparations. A very unhappy Mama had given the soldier-turned-cop a piece of her mind. I'd stifled a laugh behind a cousin easily large enough to conceal me while they watched on in glee.

"It's not often that it's not one of us," one had told me as they hung on the drama unfolding in the kitchen. "But damn, it's good to watch someone else get a thrashing."

Liam had decided to retreat, but when Joey had attempted to follow his escape, Mama tied an apron around his waist and put him to work preparing salads.

The room was beautifully decorated with orchids and white waratahs in tall, slim vases. Long strands of jasmine from Mila's home lay in the centre of each table, filling the room with an exotic scent.

Mila wore a pale blue gown that dropped from underneath her breasts. Her tiny bump was visible, and she looked beautiful. The fine-boned artist exuded class and elegance, and next to Cal in his open shirt and tanned skin, they looked like something out of a magazine.

But then, so did most of their friends, I realised with a start as I served the tables, suddenly very glad of my role apart. Theodore Black and Jenny sat at opposite ends of the wedding table, both looking slightly uncomfortable in their formal attire, though no less glamorous. I could imagine Cal's ex-partner more in a motorcycle club than I could as a cop with his long beard and tattoos peeking out from his shirt.

Danny and Laura were a model couple in their own right. Both perfectly fit, with easy smiles and comfortable in the crowd, they could have been beneath a spotlight and likely would have been just as relaxed. Seated at their table were Liam and Selena.

Micah had introduced me to his boss and the solicitor who assisted with the job that had taken up their time since before I met Micah. Liam and Selena were a class of their own, each with their own casual elegance, but together, they could only be called a power couple.

I smiled nervously as I served everyone, suddenly grateful I had avoided being seated at one of the tables. Micah was right; I would have struggled to maintain a conversation with so many people. And making a spectacle would only draw attention from the bride and groom, and that hit me as incredibly selfish. I enjoyed serving and being able to observe without being involved. Three years alone had taken a confident but introverted girl and turned me into a hermit.

Selena spoke to me, but all I heard was a roaring in my ears. I smiled, nodding and fled back to the kitchen where Mama organised plate after plate of food.

The service crew gathered in a tight knot at the back of the servery. Mama refused to plate up perfect food for everyone else and not us, so we all ate the same fare as the rest of the wedding guests.

Silence held in the kitchen while we ate, devouring the food with no small degree of reverence. The plates cleared quickly, and we made short work of cleaning up, with everyone pitching in.

"She's a goddess," Joey murmured to me. I recognised my own awe in his voice.

"Don't let her hear you say that," I laughed, "or she'll adopt you, too."

"That doesn't sound so bad," he mused, taking a stack of plates I'd extracted from the dishwasher.

"You did wonderfully, Jimmy." Mama patted my shoulder, then turned to Joey. "And you too, Joey. Though if you need to learn how to prepare food properly, I will teach you." She patted him, too, leaving him with a goofy grin on his face.

"See? I told you," I whispered, reaching over to hug Mama and ask her where she wanted all the things stacked for the return trip.

Cal had arrived with Micah in his monster, while Liam's father had driven Mila and her bridesmaids in a classic Torana. The cousins had packed themselves into a stack of imports, all with less storage space than the next.

Mama started speaking, then stiffened. I straightened, staring at Joey, who had nothing less than terror written all over his face. I knew that look because I had worn it enough times to know what it must look like from the outside.

I spun around.

"What in the hell is he doing here?" Micah stood in the doorway to the kitchen, his face completely closed.

Mama inflated, her hands balled into fists on her hips, and let loose a tirade in Italian. I pushed Joey back behind a cousin as Micah answered her fluently, both of them raging at the other. Micah's shoulders were in a tight line, while Mama rose onto her toes with a finger pointing in his face.

"This'll be a good one," one cousin remarked.

"You know he's going to walk out."

"Nah, he'll never give up."

"Shit, man. She's got it all over him."

"Ten minutes."

Money exchanged hands at speed, with Joey and me looking on in shock. Then the cousins leaned back and sipped their beers, following the increasingly loud tirade of Italian with nods and grins.

"I thought she was born in Australia," I whispered to no one in particular.

The cousin on my left snorted. "She was brought up Italian. Most of us were."

Silence fell in an abrupt layer that weighed on everyone in the kitchen. Micah stared at the round woman who refused to back down from her son and threw his hands in the air, spinning on his heel to storm away.

"Ahhh, I told you-" A commotion arose amongst the cousins, and the arguments began.

I towed Joey out the back door into the fresh early evening air.

"Wow. That got out of hand fast. What was it about?" I asked, but I had already put the pieces together. Some part of me needed to hear it from him, to tell me he had lied to me through omission.

Not that you're any better.

I pushed the thought aside, the ghost of Micah's touch at my throat searing me. Swallowing hard, I found the tiny pendant curled in my hands.

Joey shoved his hands into his pockets, staring at the ground. "Micah knows me from...work," he finally said, his lips twisting on the word.

"Work, but not as a cop." I nudged gently.

"No." Joey studied his black shoes, probably borrowed from a cousin. "I'm about as far from trustworthy and honest as you can get." He looked up and frowned. "But you know that, don't you?"

"The night you picked me up when I walked from Micah's place. You weren't following me." I nodded, carefully selecting words to offer him, knowing I walked a fine and potentially dangerous line.

This is what you ran away from.

"I was watching his house. Liam told him to watch me, so I thought I'd return the favour." He mumbled something else that sounded suspiciously like *bad habits.*

"Wow. That's...petty." The words slipped out before I thought much about them. At least I stayed true to form.

Joey's head came up fast, his grey eyes narrowed and almost dead inside. I took a step backward, biting down hard on my fear, but I had earned that.

"Petty." Joey laughed, the sound harsh in the cool evening air. His lips twisted again, sending a wave of alarm through my stomach. "That's not a word I would use to describe myself or my brother."

Music started inside, the heavy walls between us and the rest of the guests muting the wedding as the last piece clunked into place in my chugging mind, my old friend panic building inside me. I desperately attempted to repress it so I could think straight.

Joey was Wayde Logan's brother.

I knew just enough about Micah's work for it to make sense. He and Danny often discussed their investigations. This one had run for long enough that I had a decent understanding of who did what in each sense.

It was always amazing what you could pick up if you just listened to people — their stresses and worries, what made them happy.

"Probably not," I agreed, retreating in tiny, slow paces. My heel ground against the concrete step of the back of the restaurant. "Um, I'm going to head back in–"

Joey's eyes shifted over my shoulder. Abject fear froze his features a second time, curdling my stomach.

Don't let it be the brother. Please don't let it be the brother.

I cricked my neck, turning to face the man behind me.

Liam glowered at Joey, a dark, crackling energy rolling off him. I could understand why Joey's fear; I was just glad that energy wasn't aimed at me.

Liam's hand pressed gently on my shoulder. "Go back inside, Jimmy," he murmured softly, striding around me.

He gripped Joey by the elbow and towed him into the darkness beyond.

CHAPTER FIFTEEN

MICAH

Things had gotten out of hand far too fast. I loitered beyond the edge of the light, and Liam gave me a nod without acknowledging me as he towed Joey to his car. He watched Joey drive away, the line of his shoulders tight beneath his immaculate suit jacket.

I slipped my phone back into my pocket, Liam's message unread. The moment I had seen Joey, I knew he couldn't stay. Not around Mila and Cal. Or Ashley. It belatedly occurred to me that the flower girl was his niece.

But Cal and Logan had an obsession with each other, and both men had fixated on Mila. Her tummy barely stretched her dress, but putting her and the brother of the man who had tried to kill her — *and worse* — together just seemed like a really bad idea to me.

My mind drifted to another tiny woman, pictured her wearing a white dress. The image shattered when I realised she would likely never trust anyone enough to get married, let alone me.

Hell, I couldn't even tell when the woman I adored was homeless.

I gritted my teeth, letting the brick at my back dig into my skin beneath my shirt. The pain shot sharp and brief along my spine, and I welcomed it.

Liam strode toward the front of the building without speaking to me. Selena met him at the corner, her hands sliding beneath his jacket. He spoke to her quietly for a moment, then gently disengaged from her, leading her back inside.

I stepped away from the wall, still watching the driveway in the event Joey returned after Liam walked away. The man must have a plan, but I was still in the dark as to what he wanted from me — or Joey. Head down, I strode back to the kitchen. Mama deserved an apology. We clashed on occasion, both as fiery as each other. My incendiary temper was one reason I rarely lost it; the lack of control bothered me and clouded me to everything else.

A pair of scuffed Doc Martens slid into view.

Distracted, just like that.

I shook my head, smiling just a little as I took in Jimmy in her corset top and green hair. The stone look on her face wiped the smile from mine.

"Do you always hang around in parking lots when people are having a private conversation?" she snapped.

"Do you always hang out with men charged with attempted murder?" I countered, studying the brown eyes so filled with conflicting emotions.

"What?" Jimmy stared at me, but the truth was already written across her face.

"You knew." I canted my head, studying her. "Didn't you?"

Jimmy swallowed, her hair falling forward over her face for a moment. "I had a good idea, but–"

"You had a good idea, and you came out with him alone, in the dark."

"With a swarm of your cousins who would beat the shit out of him the moment I screamed! Not to mention you creeping around," she added darkly.

"If you got a chance to scream," I said quietly.

Jimmy closed her mouth with a click, snorting through her nose. She spun around, almost face-planting into my second cousin, Leon, putting out the bins. Muttering apologies, she tossed me a filthy look over her shoulder and stalked back inside the restaurant.

"Firecracker," Leon grinned, shaking his head as he hauled bags of rubbish into the dumpster at the back of the reception centre.

I held up the lid for him, taking care not to breathe too deeply. "You have no idea."

"You reckon?" He smirked. "They say you go for the ones just like your mother."

I raised my eyebrows, the door slamming behind Jimmy. "Maybe you're right." I dropped the bin lid back with a bang, following Leon inside to clean my hands.

Jimmy was nowhere in sight when I emerged from the men's restrooms. Mama refused to let me apologise, fussing with my suit and attempting to feed me at the same time. I tried to say no to both, but in the end, it was easier to just let her organise me.

By the time I returned to the dining room, people were dancing in a knot in the centre of the room. I slipped around Black and Jenny swaying in each other's arms, Ashley attached to Jenny at the waist. Jenny gave me a small smile over Black's shoulder, her eyes closing as she rested against him.

Theodore Black looked nothing like his usual, grumpy self in a white shirt and waistcoat that matched the highlights of Cal's wedding attire. His beard and hair were well-groomed — I suspected by Jenny's hand and under great duress — and he looked slightly less biker enforcer than usual.

The lights were lowered to a dusky dimness interspersed with sparkles from the very retro disco ball above. Pink glitter flashed each time the disco ball spun. Chairs and tables had been cleared away to make space for dancers. It always amazed me how the cover of darkness reduced people's inhibitions and allowed them to be themselves. The people they wanted to be but couldn't on a daily basis.

I edged around the crowd, aiming for Danny and Laura standing off to one side, talking to Selena. Mila sat beside them, leaning tiredly back into Cal, who rubbed her shoulders. Ally and Brett stood with their backs to everyone else, talking quietly at the railing that looked over the park. Neither Liam nor Joey were around.

"Hey, man. We missed you." Danny gave me a one-armed hug, a small frown dipping his brow. Cologne wafted off him in waves.

"Did you bathe in that stuff?" I asked.

Danny pointed a finger covertly at Laura. "Not my choice," he murmured with a dopey sideways grin.

I rolled my eyes. "What you have to look forward to," I commented to Cal.

"Already there." Cal grinned, his hands resting familiarly on his wife's shoulders. She tilted her head back, one hand resting to the side of her just-rounded stomach, completely relaxed. However, the dark circles beneath her eyes told another story.

"How's everything going?" I shrugged out of Danny's hold to speak quietly to Cal, though my eyes searched over his shoulder.

"He's on the phone. As always." Cal grinned, the smile reaching his eyes for the first time in many months.

"How do you always know?" I muttered.

"'Cause you look like I would have if I'd bothered to look in the mirror a few years ago. Though someone gave me a little prompt. Don't let this become an obsession," he warned.

My boss had always seen too much. "The voice of experience, huh?"

"Just don't let bias cloud your perspective. It's what's unique about you, why you're so damn important to this team." Cal wrapped his arm around my shoulders. It seemed to be the night for hugging, or maybe he just needed a prop.

"Have you and Black kissed and made up?" I asked lightly.

Cal snorted. "Yeah, we're gonna slow dance later."

"Ashley and Jenny might argue with that. Tell me you're getting some sleep." I studied him, but the only thing I saw was a very happy man, relieved to finally be married to the woman he loved. "It must be nice to have found peace."

Cal returned my study, but as usual, his eyes were kind. "Do you remember when you gave me that laptop I took home to hunt Logan?" he asked lightly, but a shadow flickered behind his eyes.

"I remember a man who barely slept, who couldn't focus because everything seemed to be slipping away. I remember pushing the laptop into your arms and promising myself it wouldn't hurt you further."

"Yeah, you're a real enabler," Cal said dryly. "Think about it, Micah. Does that man remind you of anyone you might know?"

He patted my shoulder once and bent down to whisper in Mila's ear. With a nod to the rest of us, he drew her out onto the dance floor. She rested her head on his chest, curving her body into his.

A lump rose into my throat as I watched them.

"You know you're supposed to cry at the ceremony, right?" Danny leaned on my shoulder with a theatrical sigh.

I punched him in the shoulder. He *oofed*, and this time it wasn't quite as fake.

"You're getting soft, old man." I grinned, contemplating a harder punch, but that might not be socially acceptable at a wedding.

"Piss off, I'm younger than you!"

"Really? Cause you've got the Dad jokes going, and it's not Sunday yet."

Danny made a show of checking his watch. "Well, this old man says it's after midnight, so you're wrong, Chucky."

I snorted. "Take Laura for a dance. Get out of my hair."

"So you can stalk Liam? Hell, no. I might get away with punching Cal, but you're *not* punching Liam. The hard bastard will flatten you." Danny grimaced.

"I'm not going to punch anyon–" I broke off as a body joined us on my other side.

A pity it didn't have green hair. I tracked the room for Jimmy, but she'd been hiding in the kitchen all night. The few times she had come out had been brief, and she'd scurried away too fast. I regretted asking her — not because I didn't want her in the friend's circle, but because of Joey. The asshole was everywhere I looked.

"It's not nice to punch the groom on his wedding day," Liam spoke to Danny reprovingly over my head.

"He's paid his penance." Danny grinned. He waited a moment longer, then departed. Who knew the boy could learn social graces? His woman and a little responsibility had given him a new perspective on life.

I stood next to Liam silently. Even at six feet and broad as hell, I still felt small next to him. Liam's history as an ex-special ops sniper never got discussed outright. Still, the years and his experience were worn on the outside like armour. I always had the impression it prevented something dark from coming out, keeping everyone else safe more than to protect himself.

"Joey isn't your problem. He just needs to fit in." Liam cast me a look askance. "You're the best pick for that."

I mulled on it for a moment in case I *did* punch the bastard. Not because Danny was right; Liam would flatten me, but because it was poor form at my boss's wedding. And despite what Liam thought, Cal was still my boss. While I respected Liam, my loyalty wasn't to him.

Especially with the bullshit he was pulling.

"Because I socialise with a questionable group of people?"

Liam turned to face me fully. "Because you're the least likely to kill him."

I nodded; I had to give him that.

"Fair enough."

"And that includes me. I'm far too close to this. For Cal, for all of us. Keep Joey on side; get him to talk about his brother. Open him up and show me what's inside. Then I'll decide what to do with him."

I didn't have to think about my response this time. I stared at the dance floor, picking out the couples individually. A shadow passed behind them, the dim light glinting only a little, but I'd seen her.

"And you decided to throw a snake into the pit with me, not knowing if he was safe or not? That's a trusting decision, Liam. Probably not your best."

Not looking at him, I slipped my hands into my pockets, retracing my steps around the dance floor, speaking to each member of the team as I went. The weight of Danny's gaze followed me, but his concerns would have to wait.

I carefully squeezed Mila and ended up in a three-way hug with the two of them, Cal's arms around us both. I gripped his arm, grinning, and gave him heartfelt congratulations again. The slow song turned to something faster, and I slipped away.

On the edge of the dance floor, I scanned the crowd for Jimmy, but she had disappeared into thin air. Music pounded my path. The hallway was empty too, but the door that led outside to the street swayed gently.

I broke into a run. There was far too much running in my life. The glass door hit my palm, and I slowed. Jimmy sat on the steps to the reception centre, just inside the shadow. Street lamps lit the rest of the entrance, but she had chosen a spot away from that.

She looked around as I burst through the doors, her eyes widening.

"I hate running," I grumbled, tugging at my suit pants to plant myself next to her on the second step.

"Why were you running?" Jimmy frowned at me. She plucked at my suit jacket. "This isn't meant to be an athletic event, you know."

"I was chasing you." I huffed a small laugh to cover the panic that had consumed me.

Jimmy stared at me, her fingers closing around the pendant at her neck. Something in me warmed at the sight of her wearing it.

"I'm not running away from you, Micah," she smiled. The old Jimmy I loved resurfaced, her quirky humour glinting in her eyes.

Maybe something more that I told myself I wasn't imagining.

"I'm sorry about Joey. That I lost it in front of you." I closed my mouth with a snap, wishing I hadn't said anything at all. Jimmy's face shut down. I cupped my hand around her shoulders, tugging her gently to face me. "Don't do that with me." There was a plea in my voice that I might have hated, but it didn't matter if she wasn't listening.

"Why is everything so complicated?" she groaned, pressing her forehead to my shoulder.

I slipped my arm around her, nestling her into my side. "It doesn't have to be," I said softly.

Jimmy laughed. "Are you kidding yourself? Have you seen the man who is orchestrating your work life? Somehow, I don't think it's Joey's big brother, though you all seem to have him tagged as the enemy." She looked up at me, her eyes clear, and I knew it wasn't Joey we were talking about at all.

"Logan has been in our heads for a long time. We hunted him, but we're still not free of him even when he's in jail. He's touched the lives of every one of us, most especially Cal and Mila. He's famous for screwing with minds. Don't let him into yours, too." I pushed strands of hair that glinted black in the shadow away from her face, curling my fingers behind her ear.

She leaned forward until her lips were almost touching mine. "I was talking about Liam."

Jimmy slipped beneath my arm and headed back into the building without a word. I followed her, but I hesitated and turned in the opposite direction when she dived off toward the kitchen.

Danny welcomed me back like I hadn't just walked out on them, slipping a beer into my hand.

"I don't drink," I protested.

"Have one for Cal." Danny grinned, though I could see his mind churning away behind the jovial facade. "You might need it." He nodded to the back verandah, where two men stood talking.

Maybe arguing. Arms flailed about from the thinner, shorter of the pair. I squinted, then swung back to Danny.

"Is that—"

"Yep." Danny raised the beer to my lips. "Come on. Let's be social and pretend there aren't two idiots out there fighting in plain sight of four men who utterly hate at least one of them."

"Maybe he'll go over the railing," I suggested, sipping the cold liquid.

Danny sent me a knowing look. "Which one?"

"Doesn't much matter."

I turned away and left Liam and Joey to face their demons together.

Mine seemed to have disappeared.

CHAPTER SIXTEEN

JIMMY

The kitchen cleared of cousins with remarkable speed. They fussed around me, tidying up. Mama walked out of the cold room with an armful of leftovers and trays. I managed to collect them from her and helped pack them back into the backs of the cars that had brought us.

"Do you want a lift home?" The cousin I thought might be Leon asked.

Mama watched me. I shook my head with little thought.

"I'll wait for Micah."

She smiled, hugging me. Three cousins joined in, and soon I was at the centre of a very over-manly hug. And I liked it.

Smiling into someone's bicep, I contemplated the victory, but it fell slightly flat; none of them held Micah's appeal. I waved them away and stood in the very clean and silent kitchen. It wasn't the only place silent; the music had stopped, too. Hall lights lit the area to the reception. I felt only the slightest amount of guilt that I hadn't been very friendly and sociable; Micah's friends were lovely, but I truly didn't fit in with them at all.

Mila caught my attention on her way to the bathroom after dinner, and I'd held her train bundled in my arms. In that short time, she had told me about how Logan affected each member of the team and her. I had a whole new appreciation of what it meant for them to deal with Joey. My estimation of Liam sank a little.

Half the lights had been turned on as I made my way into the ballroom. Danny and Laura were stacking chairs against one wall. I hurried over to help. Laura passed me a pack of wipes, and I spent the next hour wiping down every surface I could find. The barman shooed us out of the building and locked up behind us. I looked around at the small group gathered on the steps and realised bodies were missing from the usual crew.

"Cal took Mila home. They aren't doing the honeymoon thing, but he is taking a week off to spend with her. Black's organising cars, and Micah is having a blue with Liam out the back. He said he would come and find you, so don't wander off." Laura ticked off each item on the list, including me.

"Good bit of yelling, too. I've never heard Liam raise his voice before. I wouldn't want to be the person in front of him when he unleashes." Danny shook his head in something like awe.

I couldn't work out if it was of Liam or of concern for Micah. "I won't wander off," I replied to Laura in a tight voice, a little overwhelmed with just the few people in our knot.

Next to the three of them: Laura, Ally and Selena, who couldn't feel bland? Team WAG. I would *never* fit into that scene. Though oddly, I hadn't felt as overwhelmed in the kitchen, packed with bodies far too big for the space they had been stuffed into. These girls were friendly, but somehow, there was an expectation.

And I'd always sucked at meeting those.

"He asked you to wait for him if that's okay. Or one of us can take you home." Ally shot Laura a look, the two blondes battling over my head.

I raised my hands. "I'll be fine. He'll come back, and I'm probably better on my own, anyway."

That created a whole new contingent of silent looks over my head. Stepping out of the group altogether, I found my spot on the step and waited.

After a while, they left. Both Danny and Theo attempted to stay with me, but they had their own partners to go home with. I shooed both into the Ubers waiting for them, trying not to look for Micah.

I was half torn to witness the thing. An all-out argument between Micah, who rarely lost his temper, and the apparently unflappable Liam would either be a showdown or a potential cluster fuck. Micah loved his job, but I couldn't see him walking out of it over this. Well, maybe. Micah's brain moved in different ways to most other people. It was one of the reasons we clicked so well.

I curled my fingers around the bowerbird pendant, its shape already familiar. Micah probably earned more from sponsorships and driving than he did from being a cop — his task force job hadn't paid for his warehouse or his monster, I knew that. But money didn't motivate Micah. And the more I thought about it, I wasn't quite sure what did.

"You shouldn't be out here alone." Micah's voice came from behind me.

I smiled into the darkness, hearing the frown in his voice before I turned around. "The boys tried to stay. I knew you'd be around."

"You did, huh? And they just left you?"

"Is there a reason they shouldn't?" I finally turned around to face him.

Micah laughed, the sound booming around the closed entrance to the building. "Too many to count."

I paused, wondering if I should be digging into his life, but somehow, I had become a part of it when I wasn't looking.

"How did it go? Your talk with Liam?" The last word sat silently between us. I twisted to look up at him, but the happy Micah I knew was well hidden beneath layers of anger, broken trust, and something else I couldn't quite recognise.

"He...explained himself," Micah said, somewhat grudgingly.

"Is that respect I hear?" I raised an eyebrow but dropped the act when Micah stared over my shoulder, his face frozen.

Finally, he lowered his gaze to lock onto my eyes. "Maybe. He– hell, I dunno. He wants me to mentor Joey." He chose his words with care, an edge of disbelief coating them.

"You mean, to rehabilitate him?" The idea sat with me a moment; neither something to baulk at nor easy to accept. I could see Micah's quandary.

"No. That would be much too easy. Liam wants him to genuinely join the task force. My job is to get everyone else to accept him."

"Which is difficult when you haven't accepted him yourself." I finished the thought for him.

Micah's eyes darkened. "You know me too well, Tink."

"Maybe," I said, trying not to smile, though my heart soared. "Danny said you guys raised the proverbial roof." I changed the topic so I could let the grin roam free across my face.

"Danny should learn not to talk so much," he growled, sending a shiver straight down my spine. Rage and loathing coated his voice, and as much as I knew he would never hurt me, the old seed of doubt stung in my stomach, its roots taking hold and snaking through my body.

He's not the asshole. Micah is safe.

He is safe.

It didn't matter how many times I said that to myself because looking up into Micah's stormy eyes, I wasn't sure even he would believe that right now.

"I'm sure he didn't mean to break trust or anything," I said, a little desperately, stepping sideways into the shadow. My safe space, hiding from the rest of the world. From everyone.

But not from Micah.

His gaze tracked me, something predatory and primal lit in them that I wasn't used to seeing there.

Micah stared past me into the shadow. "He doesn't think. Neither did Liam before he let Logan's brother loose in my playground, like tonight, so he could *keep an eye* on the prick. Especially around the people that I love." His gaze fell on me.

I froze.

Nothing moved. My feet set in stone beneath me, despite the instinct that told me to run. But I had done

enough running. My head wanted me to flee, but my heart —
and apparently, my body — had other ideas.

Micah closed the space between us with a few steps,
his huge shoulders blocking out the light, taking all the
breathable air with him.

His fingers curled around my cheek, stroking softly as
my mind caught up with his words.

"You lo–" I croaked, but the thought died an early
death.

His hand cupped the back of my neck, and his mouth
crashed down on mine, erasing anything cognisant other
than the absolute male scent of him. His body folded around
me.

I was lost in the behemoth of him, utterly swept away
with his hungry kisses. They opened doors inside me I
thought were locked and chained away forever. I clung to
his shirt, letting him devour me, his lips searching mine with
a long-held need that seemed to explode out of him.

One hand dropped to my back, pulling me tight
against his chest. I rose onto my toes, kissing him back.
When his tongue slipped over my bottom lip, I tilted my
head back with a moan, letting him in.

Nothing else about me froze; no freakout, no
screaming and running. Only the desire to be close to the
man who had supported me without prying for so long, who
had given me all the security I could have wanted. The one
who had kept me from sleeping beneath a tattered
cardboard box, though he hadn't known it at the time.

Who had said–

"You said you what?" I gasped, drawing back from
him. My lips tingled from his devouring kisses, my body on
fire from his touch. I needed more of him, but my brain had
finally decided to come to the party.

"Forget what I said, Jimmy, and *feel*," he growled against my lips.

His mouth was on mine again before I could respond. Micah caught my chin between rough fingers, tilting my head to deepen the kiss. Heat rushed through me.

The wall crashed against my back, his hand cupping the back of my head to soften the impact. My world spun, up and down, switching until I couldn't work out which way was which. Micah pressed into me, pinning me between him and the wall, my hips grinding back against him.

By the time he ran his hands over my corset, tracing the edge of the material with light fingers, we were both out of breath, and I was a total mess.

"Home," he mumbled into my lips, "I want to take you home. Not here." Micah stepped back, his hands sliding down my arms to grip mine tightly, possessively.

Want and desire shot through me, emotions I hadn't had to deal with for a very long time, by choice, more than anything else. I'd thought that if I could forget, to lock the memories away, maybe I would be able to sleep for a full night, one day.

Micah's eyes reflected my thoughts, knowledge he shouldn't have. I frowned. He pulled me into him again, his fingers sliding against my scalp as he stole my air again.

I whimpered, stowing the already fragmented thought away to consider later, and did what he wanted me to.

Micah had driven his monster to the wedding, and I clambered gratefully into the familiar passenger seat. He wouldn't fit in most other vehicles, the bulk of him only just right in the monster truck, which we had *just* skimped across the line to be legally roadworthy. Well, maybe with some extra modifications after the fact. But putting him in a smaller car...I started to giggle, clapping my hand over my mouth.

"What?" Micah asked softly, his voice returned to its usual quiet baritone, barely audible over the roar of his monster.

"Just the thought of you in an Uber. I'm not sure you'd actually make it into the car." The vision of him stuffed in the backseat of a sedan next to Danny sent more giggles straight to my head.

"It would be pretty tight," he agreed with a sideways grin. "Not a fan of public transport, anyway." He found my hand, wrapping his huge mitt around my pale skin that almost glowed in the night light.

My breath hitched at the contact. He squeezed gently, tugging me slightly toward him across the cab. I inched to the edge of my seat, the warmth of him blazing against my shoulder.

My mind kept screaming at me, but I shut it down all too easily. I didn't want to run any longer, and Micah had always been the person I could trust. I thought of Joey.

I barely knew him, but something dark ate at him from the inside. He wasn't all dark to me, though; something good hovered at the edges like he genuinely wanted to live a life but couldn't let go of his past that was slowly devouring him.

Like it had consumed me.

Maybe it was time to let go of that past altogether.

I wound my fingers into Micah's, tracing over the creases in knuckles I usually saw covered in dust and grease but had never really touched. His hands were broad, suiting the rest of him, his skin darkly tanned. My exploration ended at his shirt cuff.

He opened the door to his warehouse with the heavy chain, pulling the rolling door up. I slipped out of the monster and walked into his home with new eyes, as though seeing everything in it for the first time.

I had slept in his house countless times, but each was just another night that ran together in a string of nights where I tried not to want what other people had. The security of a home, the safety of someone else's arms around them who loved them.

I paused, my hand on the wall next to the open staircase.

He said the people that he loved. Was I one of those? I traced the silver bird at my throat that already felt like it had always been there, though it had only been a few hours since he put it around my neck.

Micah's hand covered mine. I jerked with a long-tuned reflex, spinning around. The warehouse was dark, the door closed. Still working independently of my brain, my heel caught on the step, and I backed up a few in a hurry.

"It's okay, Tink. It's just me." His hands outstretched, Micah stood on the first step and stopped.

"Just you," I nodded, leaning into his arms as he moved up another step until we were looking directly at each other. "There's no *just* about you, Micah. There never has been."

His mouth brushed mine, gentle and sweet. But when he drew back, there was nothing sweet about the look in his eyes.

"Are you scared of me?" he asked, his touch hesitant, though I could feel the energy surging beneath his skin.

"I've never been scared of you. Not you." I shook my head.

Micah's fingers curled into my hair, holding me still to study me. Heat and need raged inside me, desperate to be released after being cooped up for so long.

I leaned forward to kiss him, sliding my arms around his shoulders. My hands together wouldn't meet around the back of his neck, but it wasn't his bulk that provided me with a safe place.

His hands trailed down my back, sliding over my ass to pull me into him. I moaned softly, pressing against him like a needy kitten. His kisses came a little harder, a dark promise in them.

CHAPTER SEVENTEEN

JIMMY

"Tell me to stop, Tink." Micah pulled back the tiniest amount to read my face.

I shook my head, backing up another step. "No." I tugged at his shirt, retreating to the next step. Up. "I don't want to stop."

Micah followed me, the hint of a smile at the corner of his lips, his eyes filled with a dark fire. "Good."

His hands closed on my body, pulling me into him. I squealed, wriggling as he lifted me to wrap my legs around his waist, taking the stairs two at a time. Long strides ate the floor beneath us until my back hit the low mattress of his bed.

Micah straightened, working his cufflinks loose. Street lights slanted through high windows. I watched as he discarded his shirt, leaving him in nothing but his black pants. His chest was a work of art. Pecs that should never have been so carved stood proudly from his body, more abs than I could count disappearing below his belt. His shoulders that I had seen daily in a singlet were more than magnificent bare.

He squatted before me, his hands sliding along the sides of my corset. "Turn around, Tink."

I swivelled on the bed, my shoes clunking on the bare floor, and tucked my hair over my shoulder. Micah worked the ribbons loose, one by one, kissing along my shoulders, the base of my neck. I shivered beneath his touch, clutching the inflexible material to my chest.

He pried my fingers away, drawing the corset over my head. I closed my eyes, my body responding to him, even facing away from him. Every uncertainty rushed back, two sensibilities battling in my head: experience and trust.

Micah worked the buttons on my shirt with surprisingly nimble fingers. It shouldn't have been unexpected; I had worked with him rebuilding many delicate engine parts and knew his attention to detail was intense.

Currently, that focus centred on me.

My skin erupted into goosebumps as he peeled my shirt back from my shoulders. I let him, though my heart thudded heavily in my chest. Would he see the shadows moving beneath my skin? I knew the echoes of my past were there, but I had never spoken of it to Micah. To anyone, at all.

The back of my bra tugged and fell loose. When he reached around me again, I folded my hands inside his, preventing him from touching me.

"I need–" I choked on the word, bowing my head over our clasped palms, pressing my lips to scarred knuckles.

"You need to stop?" He asked softly, engulfing me in those arms and pulling me back into the centre of his chest.

His fingertips traced tenderly over the faintest of scars, cradling me against the bulk of him.

Always the protector.

"No." I shook my head, not really sure why I needed to pause. "I just feel so out of control with everything," I said helplessly, knowing it was a crappy explanation of the thoughts rolling around in my head. None of them was particularly clear, even to me. I didn't bother trying to enunciate anything further.

Micah's breath brushed my bare shoulders. "Then be in control." He released me.

Cold air filled the space between us, and I missed his warmth and comfort immediately.

Micah is not a threat.

He is safe.

You are safe.

I edged around, the desire to *be* safe in his arms filling me, while the fear of only seeing judgement in his eyes dousing me in ice.

But when I looked at him, still squatting down at my level, eye to eye, it was just the Micah I knew.

The Micah that I loved.

His hands rested upturned on his knees, his face open and without any judgement at all.

Leaning in to kiss him, I shrugged the bra over my shoulders, pushing it to the side where my shirt sat in a crumpled pile. Flicking the snap on my skirt, I slithered out of it, letting it pool around my knees.

Micah's hands found my waist, squeezing gently. He leaned back a little, a question in his eyes. I smiled, pressing my forehead against his.

"It's fine. I like being able to see you."

His smile answered my own. "That's a good thing."

Wriggling out of my skirt, I kicked it aside, pulling Micah up with me. He tugged at the edges of my underwear, and then those were discarded to the side, too.

I traced over the ridged, carved muscle of his stomach, watching his face to see what he liked. His eyes never left mine.

Leaning into him, I pressed my lips just beneath his heart, its beat increasing beneath my skin. My hands dropped to his belt, flicking it open as I stared up at him. His hand cupped the back of my head as I peeled his pants and boxers away, tracing the outline of him with my fingers, revelling in the feel of him filling my palm.

Micah caught my waist again when I tried to drop to my knees, a groan hissing from between clenched teeth.

"Maybe next time, Tink," his mouth came down on mine again, a little harder than before, his tongue sweeping into my mouth. He drew back, breathing as hard as me.

Every nerve ending zinged in my body. I raised onto my toes to kiss him again, pressing my body to his, seeking the warmth I had lost before. Micah groaned, his hips surging against my hand. Spinning both of us around, he dropped to the edge of the bed, drawing me over him. I straddled him as he fished his wallet out of his pants, sliding the foil packet into my hand.

"Would you?" he grinned, but his body tensed, muscle hard against my skin when I slid my fingers the length of him.

As soon as I was done, he lifted me over him, urgency in his touch. I pressed my hand to his shoulders.

"I thought I got to control this?" I asked cheekily, wiggling my ass a little in his grip.

His lips twitched. "Am I going to regret this?"

"Definitely."

His hands loosened on my hips, but they stayed there, his fingers squeezing gently.

Placing my hands on his forearms, I balanced on him, sliding down as slowly, as controlled as I could.

The press of him against my entrance sent rivers of shivers all over me. Micah breathed hard through his nose, watching me the whole time.

Swallowing, I wiggled, trying to accommodate his size when I hadn't had sex in a hellishly long time.

He kissed me, surprising me with the slowness of it, one hand dropping to stroke along my stomach. His fingers traced over me as I hovered with him just inside me, turning light circles over my clit. I clenched involuntarily, heat rushing over me. I slid a little more over him, the mingling pain and pleasure there a contrast to the slow, sensual dance of his tongue on mine until I couldn't tell the sensations apart.

His fingers moved in faster circles, the sensitive bundle of nerves tender beneath his touch and the first waves of pleasure broke over me. Rocking gently against him, I slid all the way down on him, but he didn't stop. Sensation bombarded me from every direction. Micah rocked with me, still kissing me slowly.

I pressed against his hand, gasping into his mouth until he pressed his fingers hard against my clit. His mouth swallowed my cries. I dug my fingers into his shoulders, searching for purchase, for anything that could tether me when everything threatened to sweep the world away from me.

Micah's fingers tightened on my hips. He slid his arms along my back, pressing me to his chest. Those massive arms engulfed me once again as I broke, his body still rocking against mine.

Sweat and tears mingled on my lips when I raised my head from his shoulder. Micah surrounded me, cradling me in the circle of muscle that kept the outside world from intruding on our peace.

His mouth brushed over my lips, taking the tears and replacing them with something far deeper.

"I got you, Tink," he murmured, brushing his cheek against mine. "You're okay. I promise."

I nodded, fresh tears flooding my cheeks. "I'm okay," I whispered back through them.

"You'd better be, Tink. I can't have the girl I love not find safety in my arms." He kissed me again, but my mind stalled, still processing.

I had heard him right.

He stirred inside me. I stared up at him in shock twice over.

"I thought–"

He laughed against my lips. "That was all just you, Tink. Still need to be in control?"

Did I? I turned the thought over, sensation and awareness returning me to my body, my limbs. Micah, the only person I'd felt safe with for too many years, truly safe, loved me.

"No." I shook my head, smiling. "Not any more."

Micah nodded, his eyes hooded. He grazed my lips with his mouth, his evening shadow biting my flesh gently. "Good." He rolled us, still deep inside me, the pressure driving him deeper.

I screamed softly, panting as he settled his bulk carefully over me and began to move slowly.

"Still good, Tink?"

"Good," I managed, wrapping my legs around his waist.

He groaned softly, his long, deep thrusts becoming something deeper, more urgent.

I held onto him, completely relinquishing any control. My back arched off the pillows, digging my heels into his buttocks, urging him deeper. Sensation built in me, and I clenched tight around him as the waves began again.

Micah breathed hard against my cheek, pushing into me harder, deeper. His roar filled my senses, and the waves broke over me a second time as he slammed into me. His weight relaxed, and I sank into a sense of peace I never remembered having.

CHAPTER EIGHTEEN

MICAH

I rolled onto my back, bringing her with me. My tiny mermaid slithered across my body, both of us covered in sweat. She settled sweetly on my chest, curled easily in the space of my arms.

Jimmy sighed softly, her breath brushing my chest. I wrapped my arms tight around her, possessive over a person, a being, for the first time in my life. And I loved her.

An emotion that had escaped me with any prior hook-up or relationship, except for Gina — and I refused to have her negative shade in the room with us. The rest had only ever been brief and superficial. Jimmy was neither of those. I cradled her against me, stroking the fine curves of her back as she slept.

Sleep didn't come for me, despite my physical and mental exhaustion, but contentment did. I had the feeling that after this, I could know loneliness without her.

She seemed at once tiny and fragile, so delicate I'd worried I would hurt her with my great, lumbering body all bulk and brute force. And when she straddled me, I had ached to grab her hips and impale her on me. She likely hadn't had much intimacy for a while, given her history, but the woman who had given everything to me was anything but breakable.

My Tink was strong as hell and her own person. That she had chosen to put her trust in me despite my obvious stupidity and lack of observance spoke volumes. Now, I just needed not to violate that trust.

Because although the woman herself wasn't fragile, I was pretty sure her trust was.

I managed to fall asleep before the sky brightened, before energy drove through me a scant few hours later. The fridge was full of leftovers from Cal and Mila's wedding. Regardless that I wanted to cook for Jimmy, I was on a temporary high from the night before.

Pulling each tray out, I peeked into the corners, finally settling on Mama's spaghetti and creamy spinach sauce. Adding a few eggs and bacon didn't seem outside my abilities for the morning. Jimmy slept through most of my cooking. That made me grin; she usually beat me getting up in the mornings she stayed with me if she slept at all. Between the two of us, we had worse sleep habits than Cal, though his words — and Liam's — from the night before had hit their mark dead on.

Jimmy's presence in my bed was a tangent worth risking.

Thin arms wrapped around my waist, her barely-there body pressed to my back.

"Hey, Tink," I murmured, pressing my hand over hers clasped at my stomach, "you feel good."

"So do you." Surprise edged her voice.

I smiled. "Hungry?"

"Always." She pressed a kiss against my spine.

My body tightened, damned if I didn't want her again. But first, we both needed food.

"Alright, gimme some room." I overfilled her bowl and stuck a splayd in it. Turning, I passed it to her, noting the white shirt from last night had made a reappearance, sans corset. The material brushed the tops of her thighs, and it was obvious she wore nothing beneath it. I swallowed, hardening at the thought of pulling that shirt up and repeating last night's performance.

Oblivious, Jimmy hopped onto one of the bar stools at the bench that ran parallel to the kitchen, her back to me. I leaned against the kitchen bench opposite her, tracing the line of her lithe body while she ate. I'd always known she was tiny, but now I'd had that body in my hands — beneath me — I saw her in a totally different light.

"Damn, Tink. There's nothing of you."

"Did you only just notice that?" She didn't turn to face me, a note of exasperation lifting her voice.

"No." I continued eating.

She twisted on her stool to face me, her bowl half empty. "No? That's it?" Her eyebrows arched, green hair mussed and messy about her face.

I stepped forward to straighten it with my fingers, tracing the line of her chin and dropped a kiss at the corner of her mouth. Pink stained her cheeks in a rush, her eyes widening as she stared at me.

"I've always seen you, Tink." I saw a lot more now that I knew her history, but it would be up to her to tell me that.

"Yeah, well, you're a lot harder to miss." Jimmy stuffed the last of her breakfast into her mouth, slipping off the stool. She brushed by me, padding barefoot to the kitchen to clean up after herself.

I left my own food on the counter, following her around the kitchen.

"I'm not a dog, Micah, you don't need to–" she squeaked as I caught her waist, wrapping my hands around her middle to pull her back into me. Her shirt scrunched a little in my fist, drawing it up her thighs.

"I don't *need to* anything," I kissed her shoulder, inhaling her clean scent mixed with the salt of our bodies from the night before, "I want to. And I want you."

She leaned back into me, gripping my wrists tightly. "You're too good to be true."

"The adrenaline junkie who chases a high so much he has two addictive jobs and sleeps in a warehouse in the industrial part of the city? Yeah, I'm a real Cinderella story," I snorted.

Jimmy giggled, a sweet, soft sound that seemed almost alien in my world. Her giggles turned to sighs as I turned her to face me, capturing her lips in a slow kiss that drove the rest of the world back a few paces. I gripped her waist, lifting her onto the bench, so she looked into my eyes.

"You just can't be real." Jimmy shook her head with a small frown. "Glamorous men don't go for alternative girls. It's why–" she broke off, biting her lip.

I kissed her again before she could think it fully through, already knowing what she would say. That she had changed to become the person she needed to be able to hide away from the threat that no longer threatened her existence, her chance at happiness. Or maybe the girl who had always wanted to come out, but because of society's manacles, she had kept herself tucked away behind a more acceptable facade.

"You're perfect just being you," I said firmly, "as long as you're happy with who you are. Whoever you are." I flicked each button of the shirt open, but I didn't touch her just yet.

People changed, developed over time. I'd seen it in Cal and Danny recently. Even Black had found a softer, family side of himself, recovering from the scars of loss.

Jimmy straightened, her hands sliding behind my neck. Her head tilted to one side as she studied me, her thoughts obscured behind liquid brown eyes. She had always been an enigma to me, and I enjoyed being surprised time and again by what came from her mouth. It was a nice change from the predictability of regular people. Understanding people had been critical in my job as a cop in earlier days and now.

"I am happy with who I am," she said, mulling at the words. Carefully chosen words that wouldn't give anything away. "I'm happy with you."

"Just happy, Tink?" I asked, sliding my hands along her legs, stroking the tops of her thighs with my thumbs.

I pushed the material back, stepping between her legs. She moved with a soft squeak, wriggling her hips on the bench to accommodate me. I watched the movement with fascination.

"Very happy?" she offered, running her hands across my shoulders. She traced each muscle with featherlight fingers.

"That tickles," I warned her, reaching up to graze my knuckles over her ribs. I slid my other hand along the inside of her thigh.

She shuddered and jerked with the dual sensation, capturing my gaze with a wide-eyed, slightly panicked stare.

I grinned at her discomfort, knowing what I was doing to her, but I couldn't help myself from repeating the action — a graze of my knuckles, a stroke between her legs. Her need slicked my fingers as I slid one inside her.

Jimmy arched, lifting her hips from the counter. A moan slipped between her lips, sending blood flowing straight to my cock. Curling my finger inside her, I kept the pressure on and traced light fingertips down her ribs with my other hand.

Her giggles jerked into breathless moans. I worked my finger in an increasing rhythm, dropping my hand from her ribs to free myself from my boxers. Fumbling for a foil packet in the kitchen drawers, I never relented in my pace as I tore the packet open with my teeth and rolled it over me. I fisted myself gently in time with my fingers inside her as she watched.

Jimmy whimpered, gripping my shoulders. She fluttered around my finger, warmth filling my hand as her pleasure increased. She cried out, her eyes wider than I would have thought possible. I withdrew my touch, leaving her clenching desperately on air, and pulled her to the edge of the counter.

"Micah–" she gasped.

I pressed against her entrance, slowly filling her. Her nails raked my shoulders. Jimmy tilted her head, arching back. I clasped my hands behind her ass, pulling her onto me slowly, letting her get used to the change. Fuck, she was so tight I could barely concentrate, but every inch inside her body tore small cries of pleasure from her lips.

Finally, her body pressed tight against mine. The tension left her, flowing from the rigid line of her shoulders. She wiggled a little, leaning in to press her lips to mine, her eyes still on me.

Then, the little minx clenched down. Hard.

"Having fun?" I ground out, mentally pulling the engine of my monster apart in my head. Anything to distract from the incredible flutters her body delivered on the end of my cock.

"Always," she gasped, winding her legs around my hips and pulling me deeper into her.

My hands left her ass to grip the counter with white knuckles, terrified I'd hurt her.

She clung to my shoulders, lifting herself up with those thin arms. I braced her weight over my thighs, catching her ass in my hands.

"Be careful what you wish for, Tink," I murmured, kissing her languidly. I drove her upwards, hesitating when she fluttered around the tip of my cock.

She mewled in protest, wiggling in my hands. Staring into her eyes, I smiled and speared her down. Her head thrown back, she screamed, the raw pleasure of it ripping at my insides.

My own growl mingled with her cries, taking each other higher until we broke together.

"Your kitchen floor is incredibly comfortable," Jimmy mumbled into my shoulder.

I caught her chin between my fingers and kissed the corner of her mouth. She sank deeper into the tangled puddle of us, propped up against the counter.

"I think I'm the *too comfortable* bit, Tink. The floor is turning my bare ass numb."

She giggled against my mouth, her tiny body wrapped around mine. I didn't care how numb my ass got; I wasn't letting her go. I disposed of the condom, reaching up to grab the tissue box. The whole thing fell off the counter, raining soft white cloth over us. I picked two off Jimmy's shoulder, cleaning myself up. She made to shift off me, but I held her to me tight.

Her hands traced over my shoulders, along my arms. When she ran her fingers over my chest, stopping to torture my nipples with clever fingers, I stifled a groan.

"I hate to tell you this, but I'm not Superman. It might be a bit before I can go again."

"Are you kidding me? You freaking look like Superman."

"Sorry to disappoint, little mermaid."

Her nose crinkled. "I'm not a mermaid."

"I've always thought of you as one."

"Not. A. Mermaid." She poked my shoulder to punctuate each word, pairing the action with a glare. Her gaze shifted back to my shoulder, and the poke became a caress.

I smothered a grin. "Having fun?"

She looked up at me, new knowledge in her eyes of how that ended last time. "I thought you said you weren't Superman," she whispered.

"I'm not," I kissed her cheek, working my way to her neck. "Maybe I'll settle for Batman, instead."

"Nah, he's too small for you," she said, ignoring my roar of laughter as she examined me. "Did you ever consider competing? Professionally?" She went back to poking me.

"Not a guinea pig." My lips twitched as she continued her examination until I finally had to catch her hands.

"That tickles. I did compete for a bit. It was...fun. I got to meet other people I thought were like me. But I didn't need a trophy to tell me who I am."

Jimmy stared at me, her mouth hanging open. I closed it gently with my fingers, trailing them the length of her jaw and kissed her just as softly. Her lips yielded against mine, her body moulding around me. She blinked when I pulled back, swaying a little where she sat.

"That sounds like you," she mumbled. "Always so bloody noble. You could be Arnold Schwarzenegger if you put your mind to it."

The fantasy played out quickly across my mind, but it held no appeal. I shook my head. "I wouldn't be Arnie. Plus, I'm too pretty to be a Terminator." I thought about it for a second. "I'd settle for The Rock."

"You pretty much are. Coffee?" she asked hopefully from her place sprawled naked over my lap.

I didn't want to move her. Her tiny body was so pale and just her, but she was always hungry.

"You should eat more," I murmured, waiting while she slithered to the floor, searching for her clothes. I rested back against the cupboards, never minding the solid wood digging into my shoulders and curved my elbows behind my head. Everything along my sides stretched, muscles popping where they'd gotten cold.

She slipped the white shirt back over her shoulders, not bothering to do it up. A thin expanse of creamy skin was visible as she pottered around my kitchen, making coffee. I'd thought I wouldn't be able to fill the time away from the unit without a new case, but my hours spent with Jimmy were anything but work.

Jimmy curled on my lap with a single, giant coffee mug, offering it to me with steady hands. The shirt hung off one shoulder, her green hair brushing the collar in a sexily tousled mess. Her eyes were smoky black from her wedding makeup, her lips red where I'd kissed her. The curve of her breast was exposed to me as she sat comfortably on my lap, drinking her coffee.

It was the single sexiest thing I had ever seen in my life.

I slid my hands through her hair, kissing her soundly. Placing the coffee mug carefully beside her without breaking the kiss, I swung her around, so she straddled my hips.

"Maybe I am Superman, after all."

CHAPTER NINETEEN

JIMMY

Micah gripped the steering wheel of his monster in white-knuckles fingers. "This is not a good idea," he muttered, knocking the monster into neutral.

"Sure it is," Joey said from his crouched position on my pile of blankets where a backseat should have gone. Micah and I had removed it long ago.

Joey's little car wouldn't have made it to the top of the hill, and dangling on the precipice, there was no way it would have made it down in one piece. He'd pushed Micah to join us, ignoring me, and I got the sense that he wanted acceptance from the big man.

But being a risk-taker wasn't the way to Micah's heart.

The blue monster's headlights lit up the expanse of trees, which disappeared into the blackness below.

"You right there, mate? You know you gotta go first," Benny's voice crackled across the receiver in my hand.

"I wanna take the chicken track," Micah muttered.

"There's isn't a chicken track for this one," I countered. The hill climb was a hell of a steep drop on the way back down, with no clean, easy track down either side. We could only go forward or back. And to be fair, that's what these nights were about. "He's just ah– assessing," I replied to Benny, who laughed on his end.

"If you head down there," Joey pointed over Micah's shoulder, "you'll be okay."

Micah's face soured, and I could have told Joey it wasn't a good idea. "If we go down that way, we'll end up in a crumpled mess in the dust bowl at the bottom."

I took it for granted that there *was* a dustbowl at the bottom because I couldn't see a thing from my position.

Micah reached across me, slipping the handset from my fingers. "Hold onto your skirts, ladies. Try not to disgrace yourself."

He put the truck into gear and tipped us gently over the edge.

Adrenaline shot through me. I gripped my harness tightly, though I knew it would hold. Benny had chosen the hill climb, but he had neglected to mention that the drop off on the other side was the only way down.

Micah's face could have been set stone. His brow dipped in fierce concentration, blank of any other emotion. This sort of technical driving couldn't be rushed, and it required every skill he had acquired.

Joey hung between us at the back, his arms braced either side of the cab, lurching as loose dirt skittered out beneath the articulating tyres.

"Fuck," Micah grunted. He revved the engine, turning the slightest amount as the cab rocked precariously.

"There." Joey pointed.

This time, I smacked his hand. "Don't annoy him."

I returned to gripping my harness. The few minutes it took to reach the bottom safely became an eternity until all four wheels hit solid ground. Micah paused, threw it back into high range, and raised a tornado of dust at the bottom.

Whoops and cheers echoed down the pinch. Micah pulled up away from the base of the hill climb, grinning.

"All clear, Benny. Come join the party."

Benny yelled out his window as he started his run. Rocks skittered down the drop, far more than I thought we had loosened.

"Is it crumbling?" I peered up the hill, but all I got were two headlights in my eyes.

"He's going too fast," Micah and Joey replied. They exchanged a glance, and Micah swore.

He climbed out of the cab with the handset and hung over the roof. "Take it slow, man. It's slippery as shit." He paused, "Benny. Come back?"

More rocks skittered down the hill, and the headlights wobbled. There was a tortured screech of metal-on-metal. Micah slid back into the driver's seat and reversed in a hurry.

Benny's truck tumbled once, then again. A mountain of metal slid to a halt where we had been parked a moment ago.

The boys were already pulling Benny out of his mangled truck by the time I made it across to them. Joey checked the battered but surprisingly not-bleeding driver over systematically. Micah gave Benny a hard look, striding around to check his truck.

Benny gave me a bloody smile — *ah, there it is* — and held up a white chip I took to be part of a tooth. I perched next to him in the dirt, draping a blanket over his shoulders.

"What happened?" I asked lightly, knowing Micah would likely give the driver a piece of his mind later on.

"Just a bit of fun," he grinned, blood oozing in a thin stream from the corner of his mouth. I passed him a tissue, and he stuffed it between his teeth.

"You call this fun?" Micah growled, still glaring at Benny's truck. I got the impression he was less concerned for the driver than for his monster.

"Gotta live, man. What's a limit worth if you can't push it?"

Joey stiffened beside me. He wandered over to the truck, talking softly to Micah. The two weren't as dissimilar as they thought as they worked through the truck's damage. Getting it back to the garage would be an issue.

Craig finally made it down the hill on his own, and I moved aside to make room for him.

Benny grinned, diving into a retelling of his adventure. A shiver worked its way along my spine. The adrenaline wore off. I shifted closer to Micah. He looked down at me with fathomless eyes, his fingers brushing my hand.

It took me until we were packed up and ready to leave to realise my flinch reaction to touch was gone.

Dirt spat out from beneath the tyres of Micah's monster truck, the notched rubber digging itself an early grave. I hung over the railing as Benny ran across the track, waving to catch Micah's attention. He gave the monster a wide berth. Craig passed him a headset, talking him through the technical side.

There might not be any events planned, but the boys still drove as often as possible — daily, if they could afford it, or escape from their day jobs.

Micah nodded from his position inside the cab of the blue giant, waving back. He reversed a minute amount, then the monster charged forward, bouncing out of the hole it had dug for itself.

The truck inched its way across two planks, each only as wide as my hands. Benny navigated him across the pit, filled with old car bodies. The thing basically guaranteed tetanus to any driver who attempted it and screwed up. But Micah ignored the risks, as usual, and finished his run.

Benny took the headset off, tossing it back to Craig. His truck had been a total write off, but we had salvaged as much as we could, with the intent of helping him build something new. It didn't stop him from being at the track, though. "You are the limit, man."

"Nah. She drives on her own, thanks to Tink." He shrugged the comment off good-naturedly.

"You gotta come out with us again, man." Benny grinned. For a man who had recently rolled his truck, he had jumped right back into the game like nothing had happened. With only spare parts in his garage, he had spent a lot of time working on designs on this computer. "Last time, you were too tame."

"Last time, I was cautious." Micah waved to me, a shadow passing across his eyes, "You ready to check her over?"

I nodded, walking into the garage, the boys still yammering away behind us. A figure lurked in the corner, behind the roller door. I squinted, but it was too big to be Joey.

"He's driving well." Danny moved out of the shadows. I peered around him, but he was alone.

"Is Laura working?" I asked, flicking on my computer.

Micah had mentioned checking the diff. There had been oil leaking out of it, but I wanted to check the rest of his systems too. A few weeks of non-comp driving gave me time to live up to my name and tinker when we had plenty of days to fix anything that didn't do what I expected it to do.

"She's taken on a few new clients. What's he working on?" Danny backed up to make space as the monster trundled into the garage, filling it with a guttural roar.

Micah killed the engine, jumping down. His mouth found mine, his tongue sliding between my lips, his body folding around me. Danny coughed from somewhere at the front of the monster.

"I know you're there, man." Micah straightened, holding me against his chest. "You don't need to announce yourself."

"You think? What are we working on?"

"Diff." Micah released me, walking around the front of his truck, still talking to Danny.

I turned my back to them, loading a new open-source software I'd discovered that made neat simulations of my ideas once I'd logged my drawings into it. The screen flickered once, and I frowned. The thought of having to replace it brought more panic than I could deal with, though maybe Benny could speak to the guys upstairs about some mechanic jobs for cash.

"Tink, got a tray?" Micah's voice was muffled beneath the body of the monster.

I felt about with my foot, found what I was looking for, and kicked backward.

Plastic scraped noisily across the cement floor.

"What the– Tink, this is a kitty litter tray." Micah's voice boomed around the garage.

"That stuff smells like cat piss, so it works," I yelled back, ignoring Danny's sniggers. The program loaded with no issues. I settled into my gaming chair and got to work.

My head buzzed by the time I emerged back into the world, my head filled with a plethora of new information and possibilities. I replayed the sim over again just to make sure I got it all right. When I ended up with no extra nargles in my simulation, I leaned back, running my hands over my face.

My breath warmed my hands, only slightly frozen from hours of tapping away uncovered. The screen blurred a little before my eyes, and I just managed to resist rubbing them. A deep, bone tiredness sank over me.

I smiled.

This was what I got for giving over to Micah. My body and brain were already resetting.

It won't last forever.

A harsh reminder, but the fledgling relationship we had developed was fragile, far more so than our friendship had always been. I knew more about him after a single night in his arms than I had learned in over two years in his garage.

A hand clasped my shoulder as I yawned widely, the soft, lazy sound evolving into a terrified squeak.

I spun about in my chair, scrambling backward, but the only place to go was the desk. I hunted about with exhausted eyes that could barely take in the streaks of colour the room had become. I recognised Danny, but my brain didn't seem to get the message. My mouth opened to apologise, to say something, but a high-pitched keening that tore between my lips that I couldn't stop came out instead.

His mouth moved, his hands outstretched. I watched in disembodied fascination as they came closer, my heart sprinting in abject and completely unnecessary terror. He touched me, and it was like setting off a bomb, or maybe one of Micah's other toys. I kicked out, collecting him in the shoulder. Danny stumbled backward, his bulk replaced by something bigger, more solid and familiar.

You're safe.

Micah's arms folded around me, drawing me back to the peace I always had with him. I inhaled his scent, all diesel and grease. My mouth relaxed as he pressed me to his chest, and the keening stopped. My ears rang with the silence.

"Breath, Tink. I got you." He tipped my chin up, staring down into sore eyes that could barely distinguish him. "Tink. Look at me. You're safe." He kissed me once, then sighed, running a hand over his head. "He's dead."

I blinked.

One last second of peace was all I got, and I didn't have the wits to treasure it.

Years of memory pushed into the pits of my mind rushed to the forefront. Touches, emotions, scents all wrapped around me in *his* voice.

"Tink," Micah stroked my cheek with gentle fingers, "you're right here. Not there. Not then."

His arms were steel around me, but I pushed them away while the thoughts sorted themselves into their areas, all neatly categorised in my head, leaving one possibility open.

A possibility that almost broke me.

"You stalked me." It wasn't a question, and I wasn't asking him anything. One by one, all the pieces clunked into place. "Why didn't you just ask me, you great, big *asshole?*" I punctuated every word with a slap to his arm.

None of them would have hurt, but I knew I'd crossed a line. We'd never had physical contact until now. Now the man I'd managed to trust everything with — my safety, my life, where I slept and worked with every day — had betrayed me in the worst sort of way.

The way I had feared someone would be able to search me. I had taken every effort to erase myself and recreate a shadow of a person who had never existed in the first place.

Micah still hadn't moved, just watched me with an expression clear of anything at all. A perfectly blank slate.

I tilted my head to the side, thinking through how he would have found me. If anyone, a cop would be able to access all the information he would need, especially with a best friend who happened to be an expert hacker.

"Danny. You bastard. Did the two of you have fun looking at the remnants of a tattered life? At the stupid girl who knew a taboo professor fantasy was wrong but played along with it anyway, who got in over her damn head when he ripped me apart? Did you laugh at my pathetic attempt to cover my ass and hide from the world?" I practically shouted the last words.

"No," Micah said softly.

And that was all.

No movement, no more words, nothing.

He was back to his old self. Not the glorious man I had *finally* broken through the walls with. Who I had given my trust and the teensy bit of control I had over my life to in a night, in the three years I'd slept in his garage, in his house.

Just one word.

I wanted to scream.

Instead, I folded my arms and stared back at him, letting the stand-off stretch out. My impatience waned, and in my distraction, I realised someone waiting outside the room.

Danny nodded when I turned to stare at him with incredulous eyes.

"Actually, it took a lot of effort. You did a really good job." He gave me a little wave.

"It doesn't make it right," I huffed, but my glare softened.

He's dead.

I couldn't say his name, not even in his head. His face was burned into my memory, the pleasure he took in my pain, in his control–

"You're right," Micah spoke softly.

A movement shifted behind me.

Danny nodded over my shoulder and held my gaze. "My number is in that new phone there. It's a burner and untraceable. Only this idiot and I have the number, Jimmy. That's it. You call me or ask for Laura if you don't want to deal with him or me." He gave me a quick grin, but his eyes stayed serious. Danny waited for a beat longer before slipping around the doorway and melted back into the darkness.

A breath released behind me.

I closed my eyes, willing the tears not to come, but they pricked beneath my lashes anyway. I knew I had to face him, but somehow, having the debris of my life scattered in the open had changed something between us. And I was more afraid of facing that than I was of discussing my past.

Dashing fresh tears from my eyes before they could fall, I turned to face the man who had both given and taken everything from me.

The words I had bottled up for so long tumbling out in a mess even I couldn't work out which order they were meant to be in. But Micah knew my history, apparently as well as I did; he should be able to figure it out.

"You're too smart," I hiccupped softly. "No one was supposed to be able to find me."

"We nearly didn't." Micah grinned. "You were good." One shoulder lifted in a shrug. "But...Danny is better." His smile held no malice, no victory over me, and the trust I had for him held by a thin but strong thread.

My tether.

"He used to call me in after class. Additional coaching for an exceptional student. I was flattered." I closed my eyes, wishing away the memory of a girl who loved the sun, loved life, who was in awe of her own intelligence and potential. Pride had played a huge factor in how easy I became prey for the predator.

Just a silly little girl with a stupid dream and a big ego.

"You were meant to be," Micah said softly. He leaned against the wall; his hands hung loosely at his sides.

"I was meant to be," I agreed, surprised at the lack of bitterness. Maybe enough time had passed; maybe it was time for the words to be spoken. "The coaching sessions became informal coffees, then lunches, and a dinner. He

209

groomed me," my lips twisted on the word — *ah, there it is* — and I inhaled a short breath, my lungs not allowing more air in, "for nearly six months. That's all it took for me not to baulk when the abuse started."

Micah's lips pressed together, almost white with the pressure. Rage emanated from the huge man's body, rage that should have scared me.

I wanted to reach out to him, to hold him, but the words had to come first.

"He took you to his house." Micah made it a statement.

Maybe this happened to so many more people, and I just had no idea.

"He invited me for a dinner and study session. There had been some touches, a degree of attraction, but more to his brain than anything physical. Just a stupid girl who couldn't see past the attention paid to her." I spat the words.

"You're not stupid, Tink. No matter what, you were never silly or stupid. He's the asshole. Was." He gave me a crooked smile as he detached from the wall.

"Was." It gave me pause. He was gone. I could come back. But did I want to? That created a whole different part of the problem. "The first time I baulked at contact with him, the guilt started. Then, the names."

Whore. Filthy. Slut.

No one else will want you.

My cheeks still burned with shame. Burned hotter when he — when Eric — had kissed me, and I'd been so desperate for love, to prove that I wasn't any of those things, that I had responded to him.

"And by the time you had slept with him for a few weeks, he'd ingrained himself so far inside your head that you felt bound to him." Micah's voice filled with disgust.

"He became rougher, and the beatings started until he only had to touch me lightly, and I screamed like he had struck me. Pain inflicted without a blow. No bruises. And I was flicked on and off like a switch. He was an expert in conditioning." I bowed my head, tears finally tracking along my cheeks to drip onto the cement floor.

There had been more, resulting in the wreck of a girl in the picture recorded on Sally's police file, but I blocked it out. I pushed it all back until the memory was shut back into its box. I hadn't been that girl for a very long time. A time that had allowed me to detect a little from the other *experiences* with Eric, who had alternated between sweet and loving to the cruel persona he donned when things didn't go his way.

I couldn't bear to hear the judgement in Micah's voice, though I was certain I had earned it. If he thought of me that way, then I had lost the last person who, for a brief period of time, had believed in me.

"And your parents, your friends?" Micah asked softly, his voice almost hiding the tremor beneath it.

"My parents disowned me for accusing an academic of assault. It must have been my fault for being loose, for temping him, and I was reaping my just rewards. By the time I'd planned to run, Eric had successfully removed me from every social circle. Isolation meant I only had him to rely on." I grimaced, my own naivete swamping me.

"It's not your fault, Tink." Micah stepped forward.

I backed up a quick step. He stopped. Dredging myself from the bottom of the pit with the last effort, I forced a smile that probably turned out nothing like one.

"And that's my sob story. Thanks for listening. I'll just—" I waved generally to the door, leaning back to grab my laptop bag, but it wasn't there. I frowned, looking back to Micah.

"It's at the loft," he said, still in that same, soft voice but with no tremor this time. "You'll sleep in a real bed from now on. I don't care if I have to sleep on the floor or find another place so you can have mine without any strings attached. I'll do it. I should have done it weeks ago, but I–" His voice caught, "I was too scared of losing you altogether. My cowardice moment."

I stared at him, the tears running anew. "Only you could call yourself a coward and not actually be offended by the word."

"You needed that information more than I needed you. You're free, Tink. Live however you like." His gaze caught mine and held. I nibbled on my bottom lip as he reached out, tangling his fingers lightly in my hair. "But, I like the green," he said, almost shyly.

I grinned, tasting my own tears. "The green is all me. The boots, the trucks," I gestured around the garage. "This tiny little person *is* all me, Micah. I dropped who my parents wanted me to be when they showed me they didn't want me regardless of how much I sought their approval. And...I like the offer of a bed. But only if you come with it."

An eyebrow rose. "Truly? If I'm just putting you back in the same situation you've just been in, I'll bugger off, give you room to work it through. Get a girl tribe living there, whatever you need."

I laughed, my throat tearing slightly at the sound. How long had it been since I had a proper laugh? I inhaled and managed to take a deeper breath.

"I'm not sure I could ever do a girl tribe. Is that a thing? I could try, but...machines are more my style."

"I'm not a machine, Tink."

212

"Sure you are."

CHAPTER TWENTY

MICAH

"Does that mean you forgive me?" The words slipped out, damning me in an instant.

Jimmy–Sally–Tink watched me with narrowed eyes. "I'm not sure yet," she huffed, puffing a strand of green hair from her eyes.

"Hells, but you're cute." I caught it, stepping into her space. She didn't move. "So the green's all you, huh?"

"All me." She gave a self-deprecating grin, gesturing over her body. "Everything as it is here. No false advertising. Except maybe that I had a life once, and I don't, now."

"You have a life." I opened my arms, a stone lodging in my gut. "Right here, if you want it."

Jimmy stared at me, worrying her bottom lip between her teeth.

Air whooshed from my lungs, the first sting of rejection bothering me before it came. I had never cared much what others thought of me. I had my own path, and they had theirs. But this tiny slip of a woman who had endured more than I could imagine in a short few years of her adult life — *she* could reject me, and it would hurt.

Like hell.

She swallowed, her steps wobbly as she tiptoed across the small expanse of space between us and into my arms.

They closed around her tight. I never planned on letting her go.

"Is this a bad time?" A voice as weedy as its owner crept into my peace.

I growled softly over Jimmy's head, glaring at Joey, despite what Liam had said last night running through my head. "Yes, it's a fucking bad time."

Jimmy wriggled in the confines of my arms. "It's fine." She batted at me, spinning around. "What do you need?"

"Uh–" Joey's eyes darted across the space made small by the hulk of my monster. "Maybe, talk to you?" he licked his lips and to my surprise — and a good pinch of disgust — his dead stare, so like his brother's, fell on me.

Jimmy craned up at me. "Work?"

I didn't take my eyes off the turncoat in front of us. If he'd stab his own blood in the back, why should I expect anything different from him?

"Jimmy," Danny popped his head around the corner, eyeballing me, "you wanna come into the office, and I'll go through the files with you? Prove Eric's not a threat any more."

She squeezed my arm, leaning back for a kiss in front of Joey.

I felt the bastard's eyes on me, on *her*, then she slipped out of my arms with a whisper and disappeared around Danny. He gave me a nod, his gaze steady on me, and he closed the side door behind them.

Inhaling, I attempted to recall everything Danny had told me. I swivelled back to face Joey, who hadn't moved. Those dead eyes reminded me of why we did all this, why we risked our lives and our family.

"What are you doing here?" I asked finally, my voice even.

"He's going to kill me, and McNamara, he won't–"

Logan wanted to kill him. That was interesting. I wondered who scared him more: his brother or Liam. From the sound of it, Liam might just win out.

"You're clearly a shitty cell mate." I folded my arms, letting my natural personality meld with who I needed to be for this conversation. My heart beat too fast. I focussed on calming it and nearly missed what Joey said next.

"He's never forgiven me for fucking up at the bank. Hell, for being born," Joey spat, raising the eyes of a desperate man to meet mine.

"You went to Liam?" I watched him carefully, turning his words over. Joey had asked for Liam's intervention. Finally, the pieces were falling into place for me. Danny had taught me to separate intent and action, every movement telling a complete story.

All I'd had to do was ask, and we would have all known this earlier if I'd managed to pull my head out of my ass. Or if Liam had told us.

A hard lesson learned twice over.

"Yeah, but he told me to go to hell."

I held back a snort; that sounded like Liam, alright. But a turncoat could have value. I wondered at Liam's game. Every time I thought I understood it, he changed the rules. Cal shot straight; the man had finding the line between black and white down to a fine art until he met Mila. But the dynamic of our team constantly evolved, and Cal didn't hold the reins just now.

Liam was like that, using a power play to control the elements around him. I couldn't blame the man; he'd lost everything and rebuilt his life from the ground up. Only Selena had held him together. And for all the pain their partial relationship had caused him, I understood the absence of such a person in my own life far more clearly than before.

But they had worked hard together to bring him back from the edge. And Logan had nearly cost him Selena. Losing it all a second time would cripple him.

Losing Jimmy would cripple me.

"He has reasons for everything." I slid my hands into my pockets, relaxing my shoulders. Danny's undercover tricks were wearing off on me.

"Asshole," Joey grumbled, his jaw clenched.

"Sometimes," I agreed. "but there isn't a better man to have at your back."

"Not even your precious Callum," Joey sneered.

I watched Wayde Logan's brother for a long moment while he twitched, not giving him the satisfaction of an answer to fight against. Holding my silence had been my greatest asset as a cop. Perps often said far too much, and in our line of work, it also prevented me from returning the favour.

Wayde Logan didn't need any gimmes; he was lethal even when he was incarcerated. And no matter what Liam said, I wouldn't trust his brother.

"What are you doing here?" I asked again, keeping my voice light.

"I told you." Joey paced the ground in short, irregular steps, his dirt-stained fingers tapping an unfollowable rhythm against his leg. "He's going to kill me! Fucking hates me. I need help," he implored, finally stopping to face me.

Far less than a lion in a cage, this was a jackal, come to salvage whatever he could from the carcass of his brother's criminal career before it could grow cold.

And if Liam had closed the door on him, far be it for me to upset his plans.

"Then I'm sure you'll meet a definitive edge when you see your brother next time. Excuse me." I pulled a set of Allen keys that fit absolutely nothing in the workshop from my pocket and pretended to work, glad Jimmy wasn't around to argue with me.

Joey followed me around my truck as I pressed a hand to her battered body. Benny had been brilliant at getting me across the pit, but the jumps before that hadn't been as clean. The fibreglass had delaminated in places. Joey stood beside me, tracing over the sponsorship labels the needed replacing after our latest tumble. The *built not bought* sticker sat in pride of place over the rear wheel arch.

I ducked beneath the truck, reaching through to press at the crack from the other side, but it would have to come off.

"She's comfortable with you," he blurted from the other side of the body work.

"I bloody hope so," I snorted.

"You didn't know, did you? About her sleeping here," he sneered, baiting me.

I took a breath, a new spider web of cracks decorating the already damaged fibreglass. "I know everything I need to know about her. Find something else to pick on."

Before I take a leaf out of Danny's book and fucking punch you.

But as much as I wanted to, I couldn't take that option. Neither was throwing him out of my garage. I worked in silence for a few minutes, waiting for the next barb, but it never came.

"You need a hand fixing this?" Joey asked from the other side, tapping the body work.

"You've repaired fibreglass before?" I asked with a raised eyebrow, ducking out from under the bodywork.

"The benefits of a misspent youth." Joey gave a wry smile. "I used to be an apprentice in autobody repairs in a different life." A shadow passed over his face.

He needs to talk. All you have to do is listen.

And not kill him.

I passed him a rag. "You know what to do?" He nodded, and I ducked back beneath the body work. "So you have an assholic brother, huh?"

Joey snorted, and I was glad he couldn't see my face. "I'd say you have no idea except...you really probably do. The bastard's been on my back since I was a kid. Pushing me to be hard, taking shit out on me that made me mean."

Like a rabid dog.

He didn't need to say the words; I heard them ricochet clearly around the garage.

"We all have family we don't get on with. Or see. Everyone's got someone." I tugged at my monster's body in places that didn't need work.

"Ain't that the truth. And we all bear scars from it." Joey's voice took on a dark tone, "though some of the worst are invisible."

No wonder Jimmy trusts you.

There was that word again. It kept cropping up. I just hoped I wasn't putting mine in the wrong place.

"So wouldn't you know all the people we need to identify as potential threats to the unit?" I kept my voice light.

Joey's lithe frame jerked a little. "You think Liam hasn't already asked me this?" He almost spat the words, and I wondered just how many times — and in how many different ways — Liam had tried to get the information from him.

"How'd that go for him?" I asked, scrounging beneath my monster to check for any internal damage to her innards.

"Not the way he hoped." Joey's feet shifted. "My brother keeps everything to himself. Only trusted one person once, from what I hear; she fucked him right over. Won't even tell me *her* name, let alone what the fuck goes on in his crazy-ass brain." Loathing and derision rolled off him.

Joey began to mask up with tape, an area I'd already identified as needing a ton of attention. Working shoulder-to-shoulder with the man would give me a much greater insight into who he was without Logan's direct influence.

"So you do have skills." I nodded toward a set of giant plastic buckets filled with fibre. "We can knock this out fairly fast."

Joey looked surprised at the offer, but the man was more than eager to work. I studied him: sure hands working in a steady rhythm that spoke of years repeating the same process each day.

Maybe there was something in what he had said to Liam, after all.

Or maybe he was looking for a way into my world, worming himself into the unit's trust and breaking it apart from the inside.

But we had already started that process ourselves.

The wedding had brought us back to level ground, but Liam was wrong about one thing — we didn't need time apart to rest. We needed to be working together, strengthening the bonds that make us so formidable, not separating us out as easy targets.

I turned my focus to work. *Fairly fast* might have been a relative term, as, by the time we were done, my empty stomach competed weakly with exhaustion. I hoped Jimmy had taken the time to rest, but knowing the girl, she likely had stayed up designing some new car system to implement across the track the next day.

"You've done solid work. Boys might like a new man on the team." I gestured to the track. "I'm gonna hit the showers, then the gym. See you back here tomorrow?"

"Do you ever sleep?" Joey yawned widely.

Not if I can help it.

I forced a smile. "Only when the work stops."

And I couldn't afford for that to happen.

Joey left me in a darkened garage, well after everyone else had gone home. However, I knew there had been times when Jimmy wasn't the only one sleeping in the garage complex. Whether it had been a down-on-their-luck temporary situation or a night in the dog house, it meant she hadn't been alone. And the more I looked back on the times

I had seen her work late, the more I realised I'd known —
and as usual, opted not to act on it at all.

My habit of not interjecting into other's lives could
have cost me Jimmy. But more than that, I'd been selfish,
casting off the worries of the people around me under a
banner of being the listener. This amicable friend never
fought with anyone.

I couldn't afford to stick my head in a sandbox any
longer.

My fingers ached as I tightened nuts and checked
seals — I had little to do but wait while the body work cured.
I'd lied to Joey; the gym wasn't what called to me. My phone
buzzed, and I reached back a filthy hand to answer it.
Danny's name popped up, and I grinned.

"Bro. You two done yet?" I grinned, attempting to
wipe the grease off my fingers. Silence filled the line. I
frowned. "Did you butt dial me? Danny. You there, mate?"

"Micah–" Jimmy's voice was soft and brittle, the
waver at the end of my name almost breaking me.

I gripped the handset too hard, felt it try to flex in my
fist. I exhaled slowly, loosening my hold. "What's happened,
Tink?"

"You need to come into the station," Jimmy said in a
stunted voice that echoed a little. "Someone who wants to
talk to you. Make sure you get here fast or–" her voice
broke off, and she coughed; a feeble sound.

My stomach swirled. Her words were robotic, almost
like they were being read. I nodded, reaching beneath the
desk for my gun in the lock box bolted into the concrete
there. The damn clip was missing, and nausea rose to the
realm of my chest.

"I'll be there, Tink." I cleared my throat, blood
already pumping through me. "You okay?" I tried to keep

the angst out of my voice and failed miserably. Whoever was on the other end would know that I knew, and I had a damned good idea on the *who* side.

Fucking Joey.

It had to be. I pressed my fist to my forehead, a string of curses flowing in rapid-fire sequence through my head. Damn Liam and his brilliant bloody ideas.

"Tink?" I asked again, waiting for the line to go dead.

"Hurry the fuck up, man." Danny's voice came down the line. "You're late to the party."

I swallowed my fear for them both. "Be there in fifteen, bro. Don't start without me."

There was a scuffle, and the call ended.

I stared at the phone in my hand, relaxing my fingers with effort, but it was Joey's throat I imagined them around.

I was going to fucking kill him for holding my friends hostage.

CHAPTER TWENTY-ONE

JIMMY

The tiny slip of paper sailed over the edge of the desk. Putting Danny's phone down carefully on the desk, I perched on the edge of my chair, staring at the crazed man standing in front of us. Danny relaxed in his chair beside me as though there wasn't a gun pointed at his head. I recognised it as one of Micah's *toys*, but this thing looked far less fun in someone else's hands, and it definitely wasn't cute.

If I actually got the opportunity to stand up and walk away alive, there was a good chance there would be a tiny puddle left on my chair.

Maybe not such a tiny one.

I looked into his eyes and saw nothing but fear, barely covered by bravado and desperation. Maybe a touch of fanaticism. But the comfort and brief friendship I'd thought

I'd had with him was almost unrecognisable in the twisted face of a man I thought I knew.

It all came down to Wayde Logan and his invisible influence over people's lives.

I stared up at Benny, wondering when he had crossed paths with Logan and when the criminal's influence over him had begun.

"Whatever he has told you, you don't have to act on his behalf, Benny." I had spent enough time around the boys to know that personalising his name gave us a small chance of winning his loyalties back. "If you just–"

"Why don't you just *shut up*, you little weed," he seethed, kicking a chair in our direction.

His hand wavered, his grip white-knuckled around the butt of the pistol bunching muscles along his forearm as the chair skittered across the carpeted floor silently. It wavered again, and Danny's leg jumped a little next to me.

I didn't look back at him, but I prayed to any deity listening that he wouldn't try to do something heroic and launch into the air over me to take a bullet.

I had been living on borrowed time ever since I had walked away from my life, and a calmness, an acceptance, floated around me. I wondered if this was how Mila had felt at the bank, back when this all started with Logan. The turbulent, heightened emotions brought to a standstill in a sort of observational capacity, as though I wasn't really present in my own life.

One of those odd times that you look back on, later, and know that it was a time when life had two distinct paths, and choosing one meant defining your future.

The longer I stared at Benny's reddening face, sweat beading on his forehead to run into the collar of his white t-shirt, the more I became convinced there might not be a future after this, at all.

"She's right," Danny spoke beside me, resting the heel of his boot against his desk, rocking back a little. "I'm sure we could promise you everything, but Logan's loyalty doesn't mean shit. He'll go away, and he won't be coming back out. Ever. We'll see to that. Want the loyalty of a man with nothing to offer to back you on your way to prison?" He tossed a pen onto his desk with a sharp clatter in the otherwise silent room.

"You don't get it." Benny jerked, and I waited for the gunshot, but it didn't come, not yet.

The man lived his job as part of the track community, who had no connection to Micah's job or any of his investigations.

"Sure I do. You get paid, we get dead, it all pans out, right?" Danny paused, rolling a shoulder as though we were having a discussion about work. "How'd you get info on us? The systems are pretty tight."

"They are here." Benny smiled at me, ignoring Danny. It was a cold, heartless thing that emptied my head of any remaining hope. He slapped a thin, metal container on the desk in front of me. I frowned, but I couldn't identify it.

"Shit." Danny scrubbed his head. "Man, you are thorough."

Benny grinned.

I looked at Danny, confusion turning me away from the gun that had been the centre of my attention for too long.

"He hacked you, Jimmy. And probably Micah's phone from there. Or mine?" Benny nodded, and Danny swore softly. "Bloody wireless. I need to up my game, huh?"

And that was that. Not like he was talking to a man who held the power to kill us at his leisure. I blinked, fully realising how far out of my depth I was.

A clod of dirt fell from Danny's boot, still resting on his desk, thudding onto the neat carpet. A smear crusted the edge of his desk. I had a wild and totally inappropriate desire to laugh, but I held it in. Just.

The need to laugh subsided after a moment. I coughed nervously into my palm, feeling Danny's eye on me. I didn't look at him again in case I started to laugh, though there was nothing amusing about our situation at all.

As my senses returned, I mulled over how Benny had accessed the building. The police admin headquarters housed the few departments Danny had described on our way up to their office, and I supposed people came and went all the time. At this time of night, most of the staff had already left the building. But there was more that bothered me.

"How are you even here?" I finally blurted, the silence and too many questions weighing on me.

"What?" Benny swung his attention my way, shoving sweat back from his face into his hairline. "Why are you talking?"

"You aren't even part of this." I waved a hand around, not really watching what I was doing, as my attention centred on the gun aimed at me, but my mouth kept talking. I knocked Danny's nose, muttering an apology as he doubled over, his hands cupped to his face. "You're not a cop. You're a driver...you help Micah do technical stuff. This isn't you," I finished, a little weakly, Danny distracting me at my side as he straightened.

"Fuck, Jimmy, that hurt."

"Her name's Sally," Benny corrected, finally moving the gun away from us. "And I've known Wayde Logan for a very long time. Since before he became Logan. The way he is now, at least."

"What?" Danny frowned. "I mean, I know her name is Sally. We've known that for a while."

I stared at him, open-mouthed, but it wasn't the throwaway line that got me. Danny stared across the desk, his eyes fixed on Benny, and I could almost see the thoughts and options flying around his head. He was stalling, trying to work it all out.

"You looked me up," I said slowly. Benny clearly was behind on my relationship with Micah and Danny. Still, I didn't need to give him any reasons behind my thinking. But still... "Why would you do that?"

Benny grinned, his broken tooth clearly on display. "You all think you've got Logan, but you don't have anything at all. You don't know who he really is; you don't know anything about him. But he's been watching you since the start, right from when Dane got those blueprints for the bank. He knew, all the way back then, that you were a threat to him. Not much of one," he sniffed, wiping his forearm beneath his nose.

My stomach rebelled, but it wasn't the time to be precious. "But you've been at the track all the time I've been there. That's at least three years." Beside me, Danny could have been stone for all the response I got from him.

"Four," he corrected me with a crooked grin and turned triumphant eyes on Danny. "You should check the people around you more often. Maybe you can't trust the people you think you can."

"Maybe we can." Micah walked into the office, his hands slightly out to his sides, palms open. Joey wandered in behind him, his hands stuffed into his pockets. "Maybe you don't know as much as you think you do."

"Yeah, he tried to tell me that, too," Benny jerked the gun toward Danny, "but neither of you gets it. I worked for Logan since I was fifteen and had a drug problem. A big one. He weaned me off it, gave me a new addiction."

"What was that?" Danny asked, his relaxed posture back, but he leaned forward a minuscule amount. He was winding up.

"Misdirection? Or were you on the cleanup crew, Benny?" Micah took another few steps forward, halting when Benny glared at him.

No fury escaped Micah, though, at having an armed man in his office. For him and Danny, it might have been a training exercise for all they let on.

"Strategy. I helped troubleshoot his plans, make sure they would work. Not that much to do. His plans are always strong."

"You mean strong, like the time Mila shot him, and he was hauled away in handcuffs?" Danny grinned, stretching his arm along the back of my chair. He pulled me slightly backwards.

"Or maybe it was the little fight club we destroyed." Micah jumped in, and Benny's attention flew back to him. "Black was a bit pissy, but the job got done."

I snorted, accidentally drawing Benny's gaze. Micah edged forward, but I didn't look at him, praying I had read what they were doing right. Joey dawdled in the background. "Sorry. But it sounded like he was more than a little grumpy on that one."

"None of those things were supposed to happen. You were in the way!" Benny all but shouted, spittle flying across the small room to splatter the desk.

"See, that's what happens." Danny opened his hands wide, sliding my chair back slightly as his hand hit me gently in the belly. "Sorry, babe. But what can you expect from a psychopath who leaves his daughter at the scene of a crime? Who goes on a seven-year itch of a vendetta to claim her back for a bullshit reason? I mean, look, man, it all goes pear-shaped at that point."

Danny made to stand, his hands still outstretched. His feet came down, one hooked around my chair.

"Get down! Don't you–" Benny screamed, focussed on Danny as a shadow blurred the last few feet across the room. A very large, Micah-shaped shadow.

I never got to see the two men contact each other because Danny pulled the chair out from under me. I hit the floor with an undignified *oomph* and sat staring mutely at the inside of a desk, the back covered by a thick panel of laminate.

It took a moment for me to realise Danny still stood next to me. I tilted my head back to look at him, still dazed, as a gunshot rang out.

CHAPTER TWENTY-TWO

MICAH

Benny. You motherfucker.

I stared into the face of my friend, lit with a too-familiar fanatical gleam that sent my already roiling stomach into chaos.

The last twenty minutes stalled in my mind on repeat, a broken record as I assessed the profiles of two of the people I cared about more than almost anyone in the world. Two faces that couldn't look at me because of the gun waving in theirs.

Traffic had moved too slow in my panicked flight across the city. I finally did what Cal had been concerned I would do when he signed off permission for the mods on my truck: I drove along the footpath as far as it would take me. I swerved back into the lane when I spotted a sufficient gap in traffic and generally used the road the way I wanted. I didn't care if it ended up on the news; we'd probably need all the help we could get.

I pulled up in front of the office block that housed the unit, the wheels mounting the pavement. I parked slightly behind and over a smaller car in front I vaguely recognised. The sleek silver sedan could have belonged to Liam or Laura. I didn't need it to be the latter, and I desperately hoped it was the former. I could use some of Liam's skills right now. Particularly the special ops part.

I fired off a text to him, which barely got sent as I noted a familiar lanky body waiting for the elevator.

Joey half-turned and waved as I stormed through the entrance of the building. My hand closed around his throat, and his greeting died, right next to his breath.

He scrabbled at my hand uselessly as I gave into my rage and lifted him off his feet. If he was downstairs, then either he had left Danny, and Jimmy secured, or...

My hand tightened on his throat, and his distress devolved into full-blown terror.

"Message– come here," he gasped, kicking futilely in my hold.

The elevator dinged as the doors opened. I threw Joey inside and stalked after him.

"Tell me they're still alive, so I can kill you later," I grated, placing my boot on his leg.

"Whoa, man. Mech– Jimmy called me, told me to come up. Said Danny was with her." He frowned. "She sounded odd. Like it was all off."

"You think? I wonder what she sounds like when you're not there pointing a gun in her fucking face." I ground my boot down, and something popped.

"Not me, man, not me!"

"Yeah, your promise doesn't mean shit."

His face didn't hold the fear or shifty look I was used to when a perp lied. Which meant I still didn't know what was happening in my office. I slammed my fist onto the stop button, and hit the floor above ours instead.

"What're you doing?" Joey asked, reaching for his leg, his face pasty.

"We're taking the high ground. He'll light us up the moment we step out of the elevator."

"Oh." For a psychopath's brother who had been on the other end of plenty of heists, Joey didn't seem to know shit about how to defend against a hostage situation.

"So who is it?" he asked in a hushed voice as the doors opened.

I shook my head, the absence of my gun — of any weapon — leaving me exposed; I headed quietly for the fire escape door.

"I have no fucking idea, but I'm twice as pissed now I know it's not you."

"Why's that?" Hope filled Joey's guileless face, and some part of me was glad that Liam had been right about him. But I was about to bust his dream wide open.

"Because it means we missed something, and it's going to cost us." Joey's eyes slewed to one side. I glared at him. "What? And don't you fucking lie to me."

"Nothing, I just...Benny quoted my brother. Back on the hill, the night he rolled his truck. That's your leak." He looked somewhere between stunned and proud of his brother's techniques.

Fuck me, if Logan got to him, who else is involved?

"Fine." I grated through clenched teeth. "Now shut up and don't move or say a fucking word once we're in there. If you screw this up, I'll shoot you for fun and claim you were involved."

Joey snorted behind me. "You're almost as fucking cold as my brother."

"Nah, Liam claims that honour. You ready?"

"Sure."

And he slipped into the stairwell as though we were going on a fucking shopping trip.

Danny rose and waving his arms to make himself a target while he swept the chair out from under Jimmy. Benny's screams filled the room as she went down, and I moved. Danny had timed it well, but we had worked together for far too long to screw up something this critical.

The problem was, so had Benny and me.

He swivelled, the pistol held in tired arms that struggled to raise to chest height. His eyes glinted, the last of his fanatical energy pouring out and aimed at me. Three years of friendship dissolved in an instant, or maybe it had never really been there at all.

I ignored the clip for my gun that lay on the desk like a trophy between him and the two people I loved most in my life and let years of trained instinct take over.

I barrelled at him, dipping one shoulder, aiming for his midsection. But I wasn't the only one running at him, and the moment of distraction cost him an easy kill shot.

His arm lifted, and the gun went off. I ignored that for the moment, pounding him into the floor with the momentum we had gathered across the room. He hit the floor hard enough to bruise *my* shoulder, the wind whooshing out of him in a fierce gust.

A foot kicked the gun away from his hand. I stared up at Joey, my knee planted in the centre of Benny's chest.

"I told you not to get in the road," I snarled, looking past him to Danny, who was deep in conversation with the floor, where I assumed Jimmy had gone. White dust scattered over his head. I looked up to see the neat little bullet hole in the roof, glad the offices on the floor above were empty. Tracking the trajectory with my eyes, I noted how close it had come to puncturing a hole in my best friend's head.

"If it doesn't hit, it doesn't count," I called, pressing down harder as Benny fought beneath my knee.

Danny flipped me the bird with a sideways grin, still talking to the floor. Which appeared to be answering. Good to know my girl was doing okay.

As I looked down at Benny, a presence entered the room. I knew who stood behind me before Joey backed up a step, pushing the gun toward my back with his boot.

Benny glared at me, and I laughed in his face. "You're all sorts of fucked up, now the big guns are here."

Benny scoffed at me until I moved.

Whatever was written on Liam's face must have been shit scary because the navigator went white, his shoulders back and his hands extended in an instant.

Still grinning, I got up. Liam's hand gripped my shoulder for a moment before I strode toward Danny and collected Jimmy.

She folded into my arms, her cold frame terrifying me.

"It's okay," she murmured, "I've been in worse."

And that terrified me even more.

"Can we trust you?" I looked straight at Joey over Jimmy's head. She seemed to have gone into her own little world of retreat, probably what she'd done when the last asshole abused her.

I will never be that person to her.

While she was with me, she would be safe. She had to be. I loved her too damned much.

"It'll take time," Danny said beside me.

I shushed him.

"You two are like a married couple." Joey grinned, leaning on a desk.

"I'd apologise about your leg, but you're still an asshole." I watched him, realising my trust for him was beginning to develop. I pushed at that boundary a little, but it held firm.

A grin spread over his face. "You like me," he cooed, but his gaze dropped to Jimmy.

A growl rose in my chest. "Don't fucking push it."

Danny laughed beside me.

Liam waved us out the door, taking Joey aside. "What happened to your leg?" he asked softly but loud enough to be heard.

I paused mid-step, and Danny's eyes slid my way, but so did Liam's.

"Busted my ankle like a bitch on the stairs," Joey lied blithely.

"Is that so?" Liam's eyes narrowed, and he stared at Joey, who just grinned. Many men had withered under that glare. That Joey had pushed his abject — albeit rational — terror of Liam aside boded well for him if he stayed as part of the team.

Danny caught my eye, his lips twitching, and I towed Jimmy out the door.

CHAPTER TWENTY-THREE

JIMMY

Danny flinched, and I screamed.

I think.

My mind was still stunted in regards to blood flow, which seemed to have dropped to the region of my ankles as I recounted our situation to the third cop for the second time. Or maybe the fourth. Micah and Danny sat in chairs far too small on either side of me, both with their arms folded, their boots propped on the desk, crossed at the ankles.

I couldn't look at them in case I started to giggle.

The poor cop in his crinkled uniform didn't seem to be similarly afflicted. His mouth turned down as he read my statement back to me, and I had to relive it.

Again.

"Did you girly scream?" I asked Danny, the gunshot's echo not quite making it into my brain. I was still in my own little bubble where sound didn't quite make it through to me. "Are you shot?"

Danny looked down at me, a light sprinkle of plasterboard dusting his hair. "Think I'm good." He grinned, but it faded into concern as I sat there, smiling vaguely at him. "Are you okay?"

He hoisted me up by the armpits, setting me onto feet that surprised me when they worked.

"That was my first shoot up. I've never been a hostage before," I confided in him.

Danny peered at me suspiciously and backed up a step. "Are you gonna puke on me?"

"She's not the puking type. Are ya, Tink?" Micah straightened, his knee still in the centre of Benny's back. The gun had disappeared, and Joey stood, watching over Micah's work as he finished securing Benny with a pair of shiny handcuffs.

I shook my head mutely, watching him with fascination. A jacket miles too big for me dropped over my shoulders. I inspected it and gave a tiny sniff.

"Is this Micah's?" I asked.

"It's mine. So if you do decide to puke, aim for the bins, okay, babe?" Danny gave me a one-shouldered hug, and I didn't flinch once at the contact.

He pushed me into a chair with instructions to stay safe and out of the way. I nodded, watching the action unfold in front of me like a television drama, and I had nothing more to do with it than observe.

But as Danny and Micah read Benny his rights and called more police to come up and collect him, a little nudge in my head reminded me that I was involved in this.

If I stayed with Micah, then this would be part of my life, as it was for Mila or Laura. Jenny and Ashley lived this daily, the threat Logan posed to these men and their families still active, despite that it should have been otherwise.

"We're going to have to give statements, then I can take you home or wherever you want to go, Tink." Micah crouched in front of me, sliding his hands beneath the jacket Danny had draped over me. "Fuck, you're freezing." He shoved the jacket off my shoulders and hauled me into his arms.

A little warmth began in my chest. I pressed my hands to the front of his shirt, the regular thump of his heart a comfort. I removed my hands and placed my cheek there, instead.

"I wanna go home with you," I mumbled into his shirt as anonymous bodies Micah's broad chest blocked out began to shift around us.

Though my senses returned, Micah's arms gave me protection against the business of the room.

"You're doing well for just being a hostage," he said softly into my hair. His fingers dropped to my chin, drawing my head back. "I keep waiting for you to pass out."

"No." I shook my head. "I know shock, and this doesn't count as that bad, now that it's over." I shrugged. "It's silly, I know, but..."

"You've been through worse."

"I've been through worse." I nodded, leaning into his chest.

Micah spoke to uniformed men around us while I retreated to my observational capacity in the safety of his arms. I would have to speak to others soon and give a statement — I knew this part of the process too well. It was burned into my memory.

Cal approached us, watching me cautiously as he spoke with Micah over my head. It might have been offensive to another woman to be spoken over, but this wasn't my field of expertise.

Liam stood in the doorway, motioning us to the elevator. He took Joey's arm, leading him out of the room, and I realised there was more I needed to say, to find out with at least one other person after tonight.

Before we left the glass-walled room the boys used for an office, I remembered to check my chair and was pleased to see no puddle in its centre.

The only thing that decorated it was a small collection of white dust.

EPILOGUE

JIMMY

"They're cavemen. That's all I have to say." Ally sniffed, turning away from the boys, but she smiled, anyway.

"Utter cavemen. Maybe a little possessive." Laura reached around me for the next tray of pasta, swapping it for garlic bread with Selena.

Mama refused to let me serve, enforcing guest status on me. Cousins milled around the background, but largely, we were left alone. Even Joey hovered in the background. Danny attempted to help him integrate, but Micah frequently watched him with narrowed eyes.

He didn't seem content with the thought of Logan's brother as a side-part of their unit, and I knew he didn't consider the reformed criminal as family. Probably, he never would. But Micah had developed a protective streak overnight with his friends.

Possessive didn't even cut the surface with me, but I loved the way he fussed over me. With anyone else, it definitely would have been too much, but not with the man I adored.

"At least you have one," Selena actually slouched, staring at Liam. She shook her head and stuffed garlic bread into her mouth.

"He's all yours," Mila said with a sparkle in her eye as she patted Selena's back. Her other hand pressed to her baby belly. "Ooh, kicks."

We all peered forward to stare at the expanse of bump, but it didn't move.

"Micah has become a mother hen," I agreed, thinking back over the past week, the small changes in Micah, the way the boys had reconnected. Each had faced their own demons, and some, like Selena, bore scars of Logan's wrath. But each had come out on top, though the small changes were noticeable. "He went all possessive and alpha on me," I grimaced, but there was no denying my insides clenched at the thought of Micah over me, in his bed –

"Uh-huh." Laura arched a perfectly plucked eyebrow. She gestured behind her. "Have you seen this group of fine, testosterone exuding males just here?"

I surveyed the boys, all in their unofficial uniforms of black, stretchy tees that did nothing but increase the temperature in the backyard.

Ally frowned at Laura. "Do I look like a man?"

"Nope. But you do have balls." Danny threw an arm over Laura's shoulders. Her face turned red as she failed to stifle her giggles.

Ally glared at her, but eventually, the glass facade cracked, and her lips curled at the edges. "Truth. Only because I have to deal with you pricks."

I shook my head. "You'd have to, to work with these maniacs."

A pair of arms wrapped around my waist, hoisting me into the air. I found myself dangling over Micah's shoulder.

"Who's maniacal?" The words rumbled in his chest.

"You're just lucky I didn't wear a skirt," I grumped, propping my chin on my elbows on his shoulder, rolling my eyes.

"There was that one time..." he murmured, sliding me down his chest.

My cheeks flamed as I remembered what had happened the only time I wore a skirt.

"Micah," I muttered, burying my head in his chest.

He curled his fingers beneath my chin, tipping my head back. He stared into my eyes for a long moment, then without saying another word, he dipped his head and kissed me until my brain washed clean of worries and fear.

MICAH

"You knew, didn't you. And we didn't listen." I watched Jimmy dance and horseplay with the girls. She didn't look out of place at all amongst the glamorous collection of women the team doted over. But she had a special glamour all over her own, though I knew she would never see it.

Liam nodded, the corner of his mouth turning up in what could have been a smile. He hesitated, then lifted his beer, drinking deeply as he watched Selena.

I returned my attention to Jimmy. Joey also watched her, which I didn't like for more than one good reason, but providing he kept his distance and didn't revert to his prior ways, I could forgive him. Hell, occasionally, I even liked the man.

Cal caught Liam's eye over Selena and Mila's heads, silent communication between them I envied. Liam lowered his beer.

"Alright," he called. Conversation stopped, and Mama shooed away everyone not related to the unit, but Liam stopped her with a raised hand. "We've come through some interesting roadblocks in the last eight years together. And Logan has proven time and again that he has managed to integrate himself into our lives. This means that there will be a continuing investigation into each person's private life connected to this unit, no matter how tenuous a thread. It's going to be invasive, but after our last confrontation with him, I won't take any more chances. We've been lucky, and I worry our luck will run out." He paused.

Nods came from around our table, the boys lined up with their girls. Selena munched on her garlic bread with her eyes focused solely on Liam.

I glanced over at Mama. She folded her arms and elbowed a cousin who wasn't paying attention. The rest of them remained stoic.

Cal shifted. "Ally, Micah, and Danny will head up Operation Hydra. Three heads that will keep dividing and conquering until they have weeded out every last possible contact Logan has in our lives. They'll start with me, Liam, and Joey." He looked at us, one at a time. Ally straightened, still keen to prove herself, though she was a necessary part of the unit now. Brett leaned back, his arm across the back of her chair. Danny grinned, completely ignoring Cal as he played with Laura's hair.

His gaze shifted to me, and he nodded. I knew he needed me to keep the other two focussed. After our last breach, I was prepared to do whatever it took to keep our team a Logan-free zone — and if that meant prying into everyone's lives, then that's what I would do.

Cal nodded and kicked Danny in the ankle. That set off a scuffle that had been waiting to happen. Slowly, the yard filled with conversation again.

"He's not slowing down," I remarked to the air.

Liam shifted in my peripheral vision. "It'll always be that way. Cal recruited you, so there's no question that your loyalty remains to him. I wouldn't change that, even if I had the choice."

I knew better than to ask what Liam omitted: the team didn't work without respect and loyalty. Trust was a given, and it always had been, despite the differences between us. We had been fighting against Wayde Logan for the past eight years, and he hadn't broken us.

After his trials, I doubted that anything could.

"You know you're included in that collective, right?" I didn't turn to look at the ex-soldier standing beside me. "Even if we don't understand your thinking all the time, you're one of us, Liam. Like it, or not."

"Glad to be included," Liam said dryly.

"What are you included in?" Cal joined us at the table, leaning back to watch Danny and Brett mock spar.

Liam looked at me, the faintest hint of a smile on his face, and didn't answer. Cal glanced behind him at me with a slightly furrowed brow.

"This." I swept a hand out to encompass everyone gathered.

"It's a good team." Cal grinned, nursing his beer. He pointed it at me. "And I picked you."

Liam scoffed. "Yeah, and I primed you. I get to claim Micah by default."

A thousand comebacks filled my head, but I said none of them. Leon placed a speaker on the table, throwing on a song I didn't know, clearly popular with the girls. Jimmy sang a few bars with Laura, Selena chiming in badly. Liam winced.

My grin grew bigger, knowing we'd gotten through the worst of it and come out unscathed.

Thank you for reading Micah's story!
I hope you enjoyed it as much as I enjoyed writing it,
Micah is such a complex character that I wanted to do him justice.
I would love it if you could take the time to leave a review.
I've made it super simple:
just click here: IMPACT, and you'll travel to the Amazon review page
for this book, where you can leave your review.
Then keep scrolling down for a
BONUS EPILOGUE
from Logan's perspective.

Sofia xx

I am a patient man, but patience is no longer critical to my situation.

I have marked them all, in my way, after they took what is mine.

Stolen her from me.

Now, they will know my pain.

Get
A Bonus Epilogue here:
DARK REFLECTIONS
Logan's Conviction

ACKNOWLEDGMENTS

Micah's story was both a challenge and a joy to write. The big, quiet man has become something of a favourite, the one whose story I *always* get asked for. So here's to having one his and Jimmy's story justice, because what huge man doesn't deserve his very own mermaid.

My beta readers and critique partners are incredible and give me every inch of the feedback I need to extract the story from my head and get it completely on paper. You guys see it in all sorts of states, and thank you so much for sticking with me and seeing the story to completion.

And for all the efforts you guys put into *every single book I write,* Jo & Sam, I cannot live without you. Honestly. I own so many cuppas to you both.

But what's a girl without the most amazing editor to backup every word? Ashley. We're on our 13th story together now. Thank you so much for knuckling down at random hours and polishing these boys until they shine. I won't publish without you.

And to those who have asked for Micah's story and waited so patiently. He's here. And I hope you adore him.

Sofia xx

ABOUT THE AUTHOR

Sofia Aves writes fast-paced police romances, suspenseful mysteries, steamy cowboys with a Montana backdrop and the occasional cheeky god. She loves reading Indie authors and hides her collection of college romance books beneath an ever-growing TBR pile.

Sofia is a mum of three crazies and an overly large fur baby who thinks she's a teacup puppy. She loves orchids but can't always keep them alive. Sofia lives near Brisbane, Australia.

www.sofiaves.com

Join Sofia's newsletter & get a free Blue Blooded Brothers short story:

https://BookHip.com/CNMQFX

Follow Sofia on BookBub:

https://www.bookbub.com/profile/sofia-aves?follw=true

SNOW ON THE RANGE

Red Hart Ranch

book 1

Every Christmas, Red Hart Ranch opens its doors, and Montana provides the perfect backdrop for good company and better food. But this year, the table won't be as full. Eve Beaumont is a twin heir to Red Hart Ranch. She loves the land, loves the people, and will do anything for them. Christmas sees most of the ranch hands return to their own homes to celebrate. Only a few long term cowboys remain with the family.

When Eve and her brother Trav go into town to collect supplies, they each bring home a drifter for Christmas. Rhys Archer and Simon Haldon are as different as two cowpokes can be. One, rough-edged who can work the land and animals with a firm hand; the other, a smooth talker with a devilish charm. Eve finds herself attracted to both men, but when tragedy hits the ranch, romance is the last thing on her mind.

Vandalisms happen around the ranch, and Eve isn't sure who she can trust. She knows neither man is who he pretends to be — but when no one listens to her, she has to prove her suspicions on her own.

261

RANGER'S WISH

Texan Devils book 1

https://books2read.com/rangerswish

Andy Matthews is a third-generation Texas Ranger. Known locally as the Texan Devils, Andy has always been one of the *good* guys. But this Christmas, his loyalties will be tested.

All Andy wants is a quiet Christmas, and snow is building. Left to man Ranger HQ while his bosses are chasing a fugitive, he deals with small-time crimes, staffing issues and runs into his high school sweetheart, Ella Harding, supplying Christmas wreaths for his units.

When he gets the call that something isn't quite right over at the Kinland Creek homestead and that Ella might be involved, Andy heads out, despite crossing over his jurisdiction line. When he arrives at Kinland Creek, he discovers a lot of missing cattle, Ella's car, and no Ella. Tracking her into the woodlands, he worries about the coming snowstorm and a set of tracks that lead after Ella's into the forest.